To my very spe
Dinosaur Days
    21st century — Keith
Thanks for so many nice mem'ries!
            — Mary Alice B. Countess
                    8-7-'06

This book
belongs to

I got it on
March   , 201
on a saturday

COWPATH DAYS

by

Mary Alice Countess

Illustrated by
Susan Daggett

Viewpoint Press, Inc.
P.O. Box 430
Pleasant Garden, NC 27313

Publisher's Cataloging-in-Publication
(Provided by Quality Books, Inc.)

Countess, Mary Alice.
    Cowpath days / by Mary Alice Countess ; illustrated
by Susan Daggett. --1st ed.
    p. cm.
    SUMMARY: Warm story of the Wilson children and their
childhood in rural North Carolina.
    Audience: Ages 9 and up.
    LCCN 00-136033
    ISBN 0-9662431-1-0

    1. North Carolina--Juvenile fiction. 2. Rural
children--North Carolina--Juvenile fiction. I.Title.

PZ7.C8297Cow2001   Fic
                    QB100-901700

Printed in China

Editor: Janet M. Fallis

Viewpoint Press, Inc.
P.O. Box 430
Pleasant Garden, NC 27313

Table of Contents

Chapter I   Treacherous April   p. 7

Chapter II   Easter Monday   14

Chapter III   Carolina Portraits — 1915   20

Chapter IV   Cowpath Days   27

Chapter V   Wheels   41

Chapter VI   Dog Days   52

Chapter VII   More Wheels   67

Chapter VIII   "The Goldenrod is Yellow"   78

Chapter IX   The Great Conflagration   88

Chapter X   Christmas Gifts   95

Chapter XI   My Scrapbook   106

Chapter XII   Home to Fern Cliff   118

For my grandmother, who was once
Bess Woodhouse.

Many thanks to Homespun Magazine for its helpful
descriptions of rural life in the early 1900's.
— Mary Alice Countess

Chapter I

Treacherous April

Our new baby had come early, but we children were thrilled because it was just like getting a present for Easter, an Easter now threatening to be unseasonably cold after weeks of promising spring weather.

Uncle Sid, who had come to fetch us in the wagon, was urging us to, "wrap up now, for it's gettin' cold."

We (I was eleven, my sister Eva, seven, my brother Val, five, and Alex, three) had been sent to spend the night with Aunt Tess. We were all eager to go see Mama and the baby, so for once we quickly did as we were told.

I was still sleepy, as Agnes, the cousin whose bed I

had shared, had kept me awake late explaining the mechanics of how babies come to be. I wasn't sure I believed any of it. At last good-byes were said, and we were in the wagon headed for home.

"Wait 'til you see the surprise at your house," teased Uncle Sid as he clucked to the horses and slapped the reins. "But your Mama right sick now, so be real quiet when you go in."

Uncle Sid was not really our uncle. He and his wife, whom we called Aunt Sally, were actually tenants who lived on Papa's land and came daily to help out at our house. But we considered them, so loyal and loving, part of the family, just as we did all our black neighbors whose grandparents had once been slaves on the surrounding plantations.

A half-hour later the wagon came to a halt in the yard. Despite Uncle's warning, we bounded up the porch steps, each wanting to be the first to see our new brother.

Papa met us at the door with a finger to his lips. He looked happy and worried at the same time. "Sh-h-h,' he warned. "Mama's still asleep and so's the baby. Come in and have some coffee-milk until she's awake."

Coffee-milk! We were only allowed that as a special treat. Obediently we tiptoed to the warm kitchen where Aunt Sally had a good fire roaring in the woodstove. There was a strange lady sitting at our table, drinking out of one of our cups! Startled, we all stopped short, those behind tripping on the other's heels.

"This is Mrs. Bruce," explained Papa. "She's the nurse that's come to help Mama get well. Mrs. Bruce, this is my oldest, Alberta. This little lady is Eva. And these are the boys, Valentine and Alexander."

Still shy, we sat down at the table. Aunt Sally came with the blue coffee pot and filled our cups about half-way up. We added milk from the pitcher and two or three spoonfuls of sugar.

"Is the baby pretty?" asked Alex, his blue eyes big over the edge of his cup.

"Boy babies aren't pretty!" snorted Val disdainfully.

"He sure is pretty," said Papa. "As pretty to me as you all were when you got here."

We sat there in peace for a minute. Sometimes when I look back, it seems it was the last peaceful minute of our lives. Aunt Sally was bustling around the kitchen, setting some bread to rise on the back of the stove. Through the window we could see Uncle Sid unhitching the horses. Eva, Val, and Alex had a hundred questions to ask about Mama and the baby, and now that they were warmed up, just like pots on the stove, they were stirring and getting ready to bubble forth.

"Treacherous April," mused Papa, looking out the window at a leaden sky. "Wouldn't be surprised if we got snow."

There was a second's silence, when apparently Mrs. Bruce heard a sound from Mama's room, unnoticed by us, but caught by the nurse. She stood up so quickly that her chair fell over backwards. Never even stopping to look at it, she rushed to the bedroom, holding her skirts up out of the way as she went. Alarmed, we looked at Papa. He hesitated a second (he had always steered clear of sick rooms), then hurried after her. In a minute he reappeared and ran out the back door onto the porch, bellowing for Uncle Sid to hitch up the buggy.

"Sid! Go down to Pine Hill and fetch Dr. Murchinson, quick! Emma's worse! Hurry! And Sid," he added, "have someone tell Mr. Barrister."

We children sat unmoving, clutching our cups. Fear pulled at us, for we had never before seen our Papa afraid. He disappeared behind the door again.

Next Aunt Sally was getting us wrapped in our warm things and taking us out to the barn to feed Papa's prize turkeys. While we were there, a sleety snow began to pepper down.

Aunt Sally, talking mock-cheerily all the while, had us feeding every animal in the place. By the time we finished that, Uncle Sid was coming back in the buggy. We saw Dr. Murchinson jump down with his black bag that I once thought contained babies. Papa came out into the falling snow to meet him.

"Dr. Ted," he said, his voice breaking, "Emma's taken a turn for the worse. Please help us!"

The two of them disappeared into the house. Uncle Sid and Aunt Sally conversed in whispers, huddled in the yard, and unmindful of the snow that was sticking to their shoulders and hair.

Now another buggy was coming up the road fast. We recognized it. It was our Granddaddy Barrister's buggy. Granddaddy pulled into the yard, threw the reins to Uncle Sid, and rushed straight inside. He was carrying his Bible. We hardly ever saw him without it.

Aunt Sally spoke. "You children got to go in now and get warm. Jes' stay by me out of the way and ever'thing be all right soon. Your Mama in good hands."

A bit reassured by her words, we returned to the house. None of us had spoken during the last hour's events. We were too frightened. In the kitchen we gathered around the woodstove and warmed our cold hands.

In the bedroom we could hear Granddaddy Barrister calling on God to save his dear daughter who had never harmed a soul, and had brought only joy to him and those around her. We stared at each other with anguished eyes.

We heard a noise at the back door. It was Dixie, Papa's bird dog, scratching to be let in. Papa didn't allow dogs in the house, but sometimes we sneaked Dixie in to play with us.

Aunt Sally opened the door and spoke sharply, though in a whisper, to the dog. "You quit that, Dixie. You go on now. You can't come in. We got sickness."

But slick as lard, Dixie slid past her into the room and headed straight for Mama's door. Dixie had always adored Mama.

"Dixie, I declare," fussed Aunt Sally in her whisper, "why you pick now to act like this? Come on out of here!"

She tried to catch hold of Dixie's collar and pull him to the door, but the dog evaded her and scuttled under the hall settle where he lay down, determined to stay.

Just then Mrs. Bruce, the nurse, opened the bedroom door and stepped quickly out. Dixie was quicker. In a second the dog was in the door. Mesmerized, we followed.

Looking in, we saw our Mama lying on the bed, her face a pale oval. Granddaddy Barrister was on his knees at the window, head bowed in prayer, gripping his Bible. Papa was backed into one corner, tears running down his cheeks. The baby lay quietly in the cradle we all had been rocked in.

Dixie went to the bed, laid his head down on the edge of the counterpane, and looked at Mama with adoring eyes. He whined once, then, without being told, trotted back out of the room.

Dr. Ted laid Mama's hand down on the bed. "I'm sorry, Will, Mr. Barrister. Emma's gone."

The bedroom clock ticked eight times, and in those few seconds our world changed forever. Too late, the doctor looked around to see us standing like stairsteps in the doorway. Eva let out a howl that I shall never forget as long as I live, and tore down the hall. Throwing open the front door, she plummeted down the steps and out into the snow. I ran after her, calling her name, but she wouldn't stop. Slipping and sliding on the thin snow that had begun to coat everything, Eva ran blindly up the road, wailing that awful wail and stumbling over unseen ruts.

"Eva, come back," I yelled. I was crying, too. I lost sight of her in a flurry of flakes and when I could see her again, she was being lifted up out of the road by Uncle Sid.

"Uncle Sid," sobbed Eva, "my Mama's dead! My Mama's dead!"

Gently, Uncle Sid wrapped Eva inside his worn

jacket. "Po' little lamb," he said, "po' little lamb."

Reaching down, he took me by the hand and together we trudged through the snow back to the house.

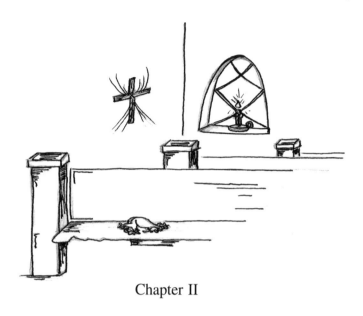

Chapter II

Easter Monday

At breakfast the next morning we were told that our new brother, little William Clay, was to go live with Mama's older sister and her husband over in Guilford County for awhile. We all had our chance to cuddle him before they went home.

Mama's sisters had come during the evening to lay her out, and now Aunt Sally took Eva and me by the hands and led us in to see her. Oh, how still she was, lying there in her best Sunday dress.

"Oh, don't she look just beautiful," Aunt Sally sobbed. She was crying into the kerchief she usually kept wound around her head when she was working.

"Look, Bert, Eva, you' Mama look like she jus' sleepin'."

So that was it! A wonderful, marvelous relief came over me. This was just a game Mama was playing. She was trying to play a big trick on us, lying there sleeping. Soon she would get up and laugh at how foolish we'd been thinking she was dead!

Mama's sisters and brothers were filing into the room, all of them in tears, and I thought it best to go along with the trick for awhile longer.

At the wake, which lasted all the next day, Papa seemed stunned with grief, and in his sorrow, it was as if he had withdrawn from us all. When we would go to him, just to sit for a minute on his lap or lean against his leg, he would pat us absentmindedly on the head and go on staring into space or listening woodenly to the mourners. We finally sought comfort elsewhere. Alex, who was really too little to understand what had happened, spent most of his time sitting on Granddaddy Barrister's knee, playing with his gold watch chain and gold watch that sprang open at a touch. Val hung around his grown uncles, who took turns carrying him on their shoulders and entertaining him with a lot of sleight-of-hand tricks they knew. Eva, although too big to do so, sat on Aunt Nella's lap the whole time. (Aunt Nella was Mama's sister nearest her in age, and they had been very close.) I dogged Aunt Sally's steps as she worked in the kitchen, making fresh pots of coffee. Under the circumstances, she tried to have patience with me, but it must have been hard, for every time she turned around, I was there in the way.

In contrast with everybody else, I was making it fine because I knew a secret which I had already whispered to Eva. The secret that Mama was really only sleeping, and very soon now would get up!

Mama's "funeral" was held on Easter Monday at her church, the Swainsboro Baptist. The snow had melted away on Easter, and now glorious springtime had returned. Easter Monday was gorgeous, mild and blue-skied.

Mama and Papa had been such a handsome couple, so bright and well-liked, that it seemed the whole countryside had come to the funeral. Anyway, the whole countryside was made up of family, since Papa had thirteen brothers and sisters and Mama, seven.

After a lengthy Baptist service in the crowded church, everyone filed haltingly by the open casket at center between the two pews. I thought it such a waste of tears to see everyone so distraught, Papa so broken, Granddaddy Barrister dissolved in grief.

"Don't you want to go now and take a last look at your Mama?" whispered Aunt Tess.

She had Eva by the hand, and they were going to go together. I could see Uncle Warren holding Alex up for his "last" look, and Uncle Whit ready to lift Val up next. I vehemently shook my head no, and pressed my lips together tightly. Aunt Tess gave me a strange, sad glance, but, having dealt with me before, she knew it was useless to argue. She and Eva went forward in the shuffling line, Eva holding for dear life onto the lace handkerchief Aunt Tess had said she could keep. In a few minutes the line came to an end, and the last sobs were choked down as the congregation again took seats.

Mr. Hardy, Mama's preacher, stepped forward, raised his arms in benediction as we bowed our heads, and solemnly intoned, "Now may the grace of our Lord, Jesus Christ, and the love of God and the communion of the Holy Ghost be with you all. Amen."

We all raised our heads. I saw Mr. Perdue, chief usher of the church, step forward. He was going to close the casket lid! I was horrified.

"Don't!" I yelled. I stood up. "Don't close it! Mama's going to get up now. She's just asleep!"

Mr. Perdue froze for a second, sought out my face in the crowd, gave me a look of pity, and, though his hands were shaking, continued with his job.

"Stop! Stop!" I screamed louder. Someone, I don't know who to this day, was holding me, keeping me from running to the front. "She's just asleep! I know she is! Don't close it!"

There was not a movement in the place. Everyone seemed shocked into immobility.

"She's going to get up now! Wait, wait! Don't, I said!"

Mr. Perdue finished; the coffin lid was closed. I began to scream unintelligibly. Whoever was holding me held on tighter as I struggled to go to my Mama. Through my tears I saw Papa unmoving, staring down at the floor as if in a trance, Granddaddy Barrister leaning forward on his cane, eyes squeezed shut. Finally, Grandmother Wilson, Papa's mother, made a motion to her daughter, our Aunt Sadie. Aunt Sadie left her pew across the aisle and came hurriedly to me. Kneeling beside me, she put her arms around me and spoke softly.

"Alberta, stop! Your Mama's gone, darling. You have to let her go now. Can't you see this scene is killing your papa and Granddaddy and all of us?"

I looked around. It was true. I had hurt everyone

even more. They couldn't even look at me. I couldn't fool myself any longer. Mama was not just sleeping. She was gone forever, dead, like others I had seen in caskets. I took one last exhausted breath and collapsed, sobbing, into Aunt Sadie's arms where I remained during the service at graveside.

Afterwards, everybody stood around in the churchyard, talking quietly. Relatives and friends came by to hug and kiss the four of us and speak to Papa again. In a short time buggies began filling with families and leaving for home. Grandmother Wilson and Aunt Sadie herded all of us children together and into Granddaddy Wilson's covered wagon that we had always loved to ride in. We were surprised to see the floor of it piled with trunks and boxes.

"What is all this stuff?" asked Val as he climbed in.

"Those are your things, dear ones," answered Grandmother Wilson, taking her place beside Granddaddy on the front seat. "You are all coming to stay at our house for awhile, until your daddy feels more like himself."

"You mean we aren't going back home?" asked Val, shocked.

"Not right away," said Grandmother kindly, but firmly.

Granddaddy clucked to the horses and they started off. The four of us stared at each other helplessly. We loved going to our grandparents' but not now! We wanted to go home! Weary with the emotions and upheavals of the past two days, however, we leaned back exhaustedly and let ourselves give in to the motion of

the wagon as it rolled along, rocking us gently from side
to side.

Carolina Portraits — 1915

Although Papa owned a plantation of several hundred acres in Stokes County, he never farmed it himself, preferring to rent the land to sharecroppers. He was in the lumber business instead, and made a good living supplying crossties for the Norfolk and Western Railroad. He generally had several sawmills going at once in different parts of the county, and was often gone from home for days at a time overseeing these.

Part of his job was "cruising the timber," riding on horseback through timber tracts to see how much and what kind of lumber could be cut out. Sometimes I was allowed to go along, and I grew to love riding so much that for my eighth birthday, Papa gave me a horse of my own. She was a gentle gray I called Nell. It wasn't long before I was earning twenty cents a week delivering "Grit" magazine on Nell's back to neighbors.

I was always a headstrong child, and I must have given all my elders plenty of vexation. One of my chief delights was to run away down the road to play with the Hutchins children. There were about ten of them, completely happy in their unwashed state, and to me they seemed much more imaginative and inventive at play than my other friends. But Aunt Sally would always come after me with a switch, flicking at my legs with it, and fussing the whole way home about my playing with them.

I remember my hardest spanking was for what I did once when Mama sent me to the store in Pine Hill for some cheese and crackers. Inside the store I became enamored of a cunning suite of toy parlor furniture: a wooden table with four chairs and a red velvet settee. I used Mama's change to buy it, then, growing hungry on the way home, polished off all the cheese and crackers as well.

Every Sunday after church, our family went to Granddaddy Wilson's for dinner. Grandmother would feed not only her eight children still at home, but also the married children and their offspring who came regularly. After our repast, while the women washed up and the men sat around discussing crops, we children would begin our play. The game we liked best was what some children called Hide-and-Seek, but we called Boogieman, possibly to make it even scarier. On summer evenings with the dark coming on and our young aunts and uncles fueling our imaginations, the game could turn into an exercise in terror. Once Eva actually fainted where she was hiding in some weeds. Always at the close of the day when the time came for us to leave and we would hear Mama calling us, we would do anything to get to stay a while longer.

'Hide, hide!" Aunt Delia would urge. (She was my aunt, but exactly my age, which we thought hilarious.)

And Eva and I would crouch down amongst the springy foliage of the boxwoods that grew at the side of the house, hoping that the search for us would be given up and we could go on playing.

During the summer months when we had no school, we got to spend whole weeks at Granddaddy's. And if there was a shortage of bed space due to company, we were allowed the best treat of all — sleeping on the floor on a quilt pallet. Lying as close to the window as possible on hot summer nights, Aunt Delia and Eva and I would invariably fall into fits of helpless giggling. Then Granddaddy would rap on the ceiling beneath us with his cane (in the winter with a poker) and we would immediately get very quiet.

It was said that Granddaddy Wilson had led a wild youth. He had supposedly embraced all the vices: chawed tobacco, cussed, drunk corn whiskey, danced and played the banjo on Sunday. On a Sunday in his twenty-fifth year he had wickedly spent the entire Sabbath playing the banjo and dancing. That night the Devil came to him in a dream and locked him into heavy chains, prior to leading him down to Hell. When he awoke, he was so glad to find this was just a dream that he repented of all his sins and joined the church. He was a Born-Again Christian, very stern and unbending, and we were properly terrified of him. Physically, he was scary also with his long white beard and piercing blue eyes. I thought he looked just like the picture of Moses in our family Bible.

Grandmother Wilson was of Pennsylvania Dutch extraction. Reputedly, her mother had once lived an easy life with slaves to wait upon her. But at the close of the War Between the States, her soldier husband had never come home, and she and her three children had to go live with cousins who treated them like servants. Great-grandmother was said to have taken to her bed, refusing to get up again. Our grandmother had married at fourteen, perhaps to escape this sad situation.

Granddaddy and Grandmother had fourteen children, eight sons and six daughters. Our Papa, William Albert, was the oldest. The next five— Uncle Henry, Aunt Dora, Aunt Tess, Uncle Rupert, and Uncle Dodd — were married and living with their families in the countryside surrounding Pine Hill. The rest were still at home, giving us lots of company. There was Uncle Whitney, a handsome bachelor of twenty-four, and Aunt Sadie, who, it looked like, would never marry because she had been bitten by a copperhead at age twelve, and after that had never grown. She was not much taller than we, but carried herself with such dignity that we never forgot she was our aunt and not our playmate. It was Aunt Sadie who helped us with our school lessons, heard our bedtime prayers, and in many other ways gave the most time to us. Next were two sets of "near-twins' — Uncles Warren and Wright, and Aunts Molly and Martha — all born at ten months intervals; they stuck together like glue.

Last were the uncle and aunt nearest our age: Arthur, twelve, and Delia, eleven. Of course, it was with them that we spent the most time.

As we rolled along in the covered wagon bound for Granddaddy's that sad Easter Monday, I was thinking back on how little there had been to trouble me in the quiet past, beyond my occasional falls from grace and resulting punishments, and the natural jealousy I experienced from having to share Mama and Papa with my siblings. What lay ahead for me now? What lay ahead for all of us, I wondered. Why couldn't we be with Papa? Why couldn't we go home?

Now we reached the Cedar Row, what everyone called the two lines of tall cedar trees that edged the drive up to Granddaddy's. Here Delia, Eva, and I often played with our dolls and made playhouses. Beyond Grandmother's shoulders I now glimpsed the familiar white frame house with the red tin roof on which we loved to hear the rain beat. The wagon came to a halt in the yard and we clambered down. Val and Alex were whisked away at once by solicitous uncles. Eva and I were put in the charge of Aunt Sadie who suggested we look at the stereoscope slides in the parlor. Everyone seemed bent on keeping us occupied.

It wasn't long before Grandmother announced supper, and we filed into the huge kitchen that also served as the dining place. Granddaddy Wilson was already in his chair at one end of the long table. Grandmother Wilson sat down at the other end, and we young folk quickly filled up the two benches on either side. Eva and I had to do some fast jockeying in the crowd as we always tried to get as close to Grandmother (and as far away from Granddaddy) as possible.

Now Granddaddy bowed his head and cried out his usual "Oh, God."' Beyond those first two words his grace deteriorated into a jumble of words that no one had ever been able to figure out. Grandmother began to pass around bowls of cream gravy sprinkled with chopped egg, and plates of hot biscuits. We had buttermilk to drink and, as always, plenty of freshly-churned butter and molasses to put on our bread. Granddaddy did not allow conversation at the table, so the only sound for awhile was the snap of the fire in the monstrous fireplace at one side of the room and the polite scrape of our cutlery.

When we had finished our meal Eva and I did as Mama had taught us and neatly folded our napkins, the ones Grandmother and our aunts made out of worn-out tablecloths. Mine was edged with a band of crochet-work for decoration, and I remembered that Grandmother had promised to show Eva and me how to do it.

Granddaddy pushed his chair back from the table and stood up.

"Sadie," he said, "we'll have family worship in the parlor."

Aunt Molly and Aunt Martha stayed to help Grandmother clear the table and wash up, but the rest of us crowded into the parlor where Aunt Sadie, always in charge of these gatherings, was seated at the organ. We sang "Blest Be the Ties that Bind," and Aunt Sadie read from the big family Bible.

Lastly, Granddaddy stood up in the middle of the room to pray. Silencing with a severe look a scuffle between Val and Uncle Art over in the corner, he bowed his head, leaned on his cane, and began, "Oh, Lord, look down in tender love on us tonight as we open our home and our hearts to these little souls who have lost their mother. Heal their sorrow, we beseech Thee. Give us the grace and charity to shepherd them in Your paths, as Ye would have us do. In His name we pray, Amen."

We all looked up.

"This has been a long and taxing day," declared Granddaddy. "We'll retire early."

The youngsters of the family knew they were meant to go straight up without dawdling, and so obediently we climbed the stairs.

Upstairs, Granddaddy's house consisted of three rooms: the boys' room, or, as he called it, the bachelors' dormitory; the girls' room, or according to Granddaddy, the spinsters' dormitory; and the company bedroom where the visiting married couples stayed.

As Delia, Eva, and I bedded down silently in our corner of the girls' room, there were none of the customary giggles to break the gloom of that grievous night.

Chapter IV

Cowpath Days

I wheedled at Grandmother all the next day, pleading that Eva and I be excused from attending school for the rest of the year. We had never gone to the public school in nearby Pine Hill. Instead, Papa had arranged for us to be taught in Mrs. Phifer's home with her three children and three of our cousins. Mrs. Phifer, a former schoolteacher, was now a widow with a big plantation to maintain, and Papa felt that not only did she need the money, but also that we would benefit from the private instruction. Anyway, since it was only a matter of two weeks and she felt sorry for us, Grandmother finally agreed.

It might have been easier had we gone on to school, for Grandmother believed idle hands to be "tools of the devil," and each morning after breakfast she put us straight to work.

First, we helped Aunt Sadie make the beds; then we were sent outside with brush brooms to sweep the dooryards. By the time we finished we felt we had done an acre or more. Our next chore was to go with Aunt Sadie to the henhouse to feed the chickens, turkeys, ducks, and guineas.

While Aunt Sadie fed the fowl, Eva, Val and I were supposed to search out turkey-hen nests (as Grandmother wanted eggs, not more turkeys). The turkey-hens were so secretive that it was like sending us to find a real needle in a real haystack. Sometimes we would spy out a nest with a half-dozen eggs or so in a dense hedgerow or under the corner of a low building. It made us want to wring their skinny necks when, after we had searched so long and hard, the turkey-hens would come strutting proudly across the barnyard, parading a long string of family.

We were glad when Pine Hill School let out, for then Delia and Art were free to be with us all day. As the May days gave way to June and summer, it appeared our main task in life from now on was going to be minding the cows. Granddaddy Wilson sent us off each dewy morning, warning us not to let the cows get into the wheat. The wheat had only another few weeks to go until maturity and threshing-time, and it was literally bread out of our mouths to let the cows graze in the wheat-fields now. Even worse than letting the cows get into *our* wheat, according to Granddaddy, was letting the cows get into our *neighbor's* wheat. He acted as if that were the eighth deadly sin.

Our band was usually composed of Delia, Art, Eva, and me, and only occasionally Val, as he more often chose to play at the house with Alex.

It was not far into June when we were befriended by a

"poor unfortunate" (as Delia insisted on calling her) from one of the farms down the road. Gerda Hamner was about our age, but so slow-moving and deliberate at everything that Art swore she had molasses in her veins. She was from a family of twelve children, and we decided that her dazed look of happiness was from the surprise of escaping the crowd at her house and getting to join us. It was soon obvious she worshiped us, and would move heaven and earth to be with us. Gerda was always there waiting, patient as the cows, when we burst out of the house each morning after breakfast.

And so off after our cows we would go, trotting light-heartedly down the cowpath through the pasture, past the stable where the mules and horses were lodged, past strung spiderwebs beaded with dew, past buttercups glinting in the sun like new money.

Granddaddy had four cows, all Guernseys because he said they gave the richest milk. The cows were named Queenie (because she was the boss), May (because she was born in May), Iris (because she had once eaten up Grandmother's prize irises), and Pat (named that when Granddaddy bought her).

Art would drive the cows before him with a thin switch. Queenie, a cowbell around her neck so that we could keep track of our herd, always had to be out front, and would swiftly nose aside the other three if she wasn't given that position. Art, his deep-red hair almost the same color as the hides, would be switching at their rumps, grumbling at them and us, too.

"Come on, girls, you're supposed to be helping me, you know. I can't do everything by myself," he would nag even if we slowed down to get stones out of our shoes.

For some magical reason one leg of Art's knee pants was always hanging low, the buckle either undone or broken. And the other pant leg was forever twisted. Art was the kind of person who would look untidy laid out for burial.

Behind Art would come Delia with her light strawberry-blonde hair braided and coiled entrancingly around her wide forehead. Even in a dress of faded blue chambray (ordered by the bolt from Sears, Roebuck) Delia had a serene beauty I secretly coveted. She had even had the good fortune not to inherit the family freckles. Eva and I looked more like our Mama's side of the family, with the same hazel eyes and thick curly hair that we detested because it defied braiding.

Last of all came Gerda wearing whatever garment her hand had fallen on first that morning. One day she would appear in a dress that obviously belonged to an older sister, so long it would be dragging the ground and catching on weeds. The next day she might wear her brother's bib overalls. Art swore Gerda's mother cut her hair by putting a funnel on top of her head and whacking off everything that stuck out. Her hair certainly did have peculiar angles to it, straight and short as it was. And since we never saw her in shoes all summer we had to conclude that her feet were impervious to pain. Without a word of protest, without even flinching, Gerda could walk over rocky creek beds, fields of sharp stubble, or hot sand in a roadbed. She reminded me of those Indian fakirs who can sleep on beds of nails. I thought Gerda must have known some of their secrets.

Once we had located our herd, where they were usually pulling peacefully at some permissible forage, we would launch our day of play. Eva liked to make playhouses in the edge of the woods, and we would help her, first outlining the rooms with clumps of moss, then furnishing them with flat-rock tables and chairs. We dined using acorn cups as bowls and leaves as plates. Sticks were our forks and knives. We even made clothes for ourselves by joining leaves together with thorns.

Art was always the father, Delia the mother, Eva the baby, and Gerda and I took varying supporting roles. After a while this grew boring (except to Eva) and we looked around for other things to do.

Tree-climbing became our new diversion. (Admittedly, we didn't worry much about the cows.) Art was expert at spotting trees that were climbable.

"Here's a good one," we would hear him holler from the quarter of the woods he was searching, and we would run to find him. In a minute we would be swarming up and down and all over the tree he had discovered.

One morning we sighted a likely-looking sycamore, the trunk of which divided about four feet off the ground into two sturdy limbs with lots of spreading branches to clamber on.

"That looks like a good one," decided Art, "but I wonder if those upper branches will hold us." He turned to Gerda. "You're heavier than we are, Gerda. If that tree holds you, it'll hold us. You climb up and be the tester."

Obediently Gerda began to climb the tree. We watched serenely from below as our "tester" got higher and higher. She was almost at tiptop when we heard an ominous snap, and Gerda began plummeting earthward, her fall broken every foot or so along the way by popping branches. Down, down she came in a shower of twigs as we watched open-mouthed from below. Then several feet off the ground where the trunk divided, Gerda abruptly lodged, wedged in the crotch. Horrified, we rushed to her aid. It took all our combined strength and engineering to extract Gerda from the tree-crotch to freedom. Frightened that we had caused her fatal harm, we lowered her to the ground. "Gerda," asked Art anxiously, "are you still alive?"

"That tree won't hold you in the top," replied the dazed girl.

Surprisingly Gerda seemed none the worse for her fall. But Delia worried to me in whispers all afternoon, afraid that the sudden jolt might have sprained her brain.

✦ ✦ ✦ ✦ ✦ ✦ ✦ ✦ ✦ ✦

As the summer days heated up, our cows quite naturally began to graze in the cooler environs of the Dan River. We were even more pleased with our new surroundings than the cows, for here there were new and more interesting things to do.

The banks of the river were shady and pleasant with patches of fern. The woods at the sandy bank edge were draped with wild grape vines, some as thick as our arms. We had heard the boys of the family talk about fun swinging on vines, and we wanted to try it. We searched diligently all one morning and finally settled on a strong-looking length looped from one big tree to another across a little hollow that ran down to the river's edge. We figured on a good long ride if we could free the loop about halfway up the far tree, bring the free end back to the near tree, and swing ourselves out over the hollow.

Art waded into the river and got a thin, sharp rock to use for cutting the vine in two. Climbing up the far tree, he sawed back and forth at the tough wood until it separated. The long free piece swung back across the hollow and hung there invitingly.

"Hooray!" we all cried. We were ready for some real fun.

"Now," said Art, shinnying back down the tree, "who's going to be the first to try our swing?" He looked around expectantly and his eye fell on Gerda.

"Gerda," he started out, "you can be the tester and..."

"Oh, no, you don't, Art," exclaimed Delia. "You're not picking Gerda this time!"

"All right, all right," muttered Art.

But Gerda, puppy-dog eager to please us, was already galloping across the hollow. Now she was reaching for the end of the vine. Even as Delia shouted for her to wait, Gerda grabbed it high up and took a deep breath.

"Gerda!" yelled Delia, "Don't you move! We're coming!"

We started over to her, but before we went three steps Gerda backed up, ran forward, and sailed out into space. For a moment her ride looked magnificent; then something odd happened. We hadn't calculated on how twisted the vine was, and somehow, as Gerda soared, it curved her slowly but steadily around in a wide semicircle that sent her, not over the hollow, but over the river instead.

"Would you look at that?" said Art admiringly as Gerda flew gracefully out over the water. Then at the very height of her flight, there was a wrenching sound as the vine tore loose from the tree, and we watched in awe as Gerda, still clutching the broken length, plunged straight down into the Dan below.

"By George," exclaimed Art proudly, "she's done it again!"

Terrified that Gerda really was a goner this time, we rushed to the bank and scanned the surface of the pool into which she had disappeared. It seemed forever, but in a second Gerda surfaced, gasping for air and spewing out a mixture of water and sand.

We waded in and pushed and pulled the soaked, bewildered girl back to the bank where she lay spitting and coughing for a long time before she could speak.

"That vine rides pretty good," she managed to choke out.

Delia wouldn't speak to Art for the rest of the day. She offered to walk Gerda home for a change of clothes, but in the summer heat she dried out in no time.

"Gerda," comforted Delia with her arm around the luckless girl, "you are our true friend."

Wisely deciding to let the vine swing idea go for awhile, we amused ourselves in the damp sand on the river bank, burying our feet in it and carefully withdrawing them to create what we called "toad houses." One day we made a whole city of toad houses with a maze of connecting streets, but this occupation was beginning to pall.

"I know," said Art in his by-now-familiar "bright-idea" voice, "let's have a funeral. We can bury someone in the sand and hold a service over the grave. One of us can be the preacher and the rest can be the mourners. It'll be fun!"

"You are not burying Gerda!" hissed Delia.

"I wasn't going to," returned Art blandly. "We need someone little 'cause this'll be a lot of hard work."

His eager eye fell on Eva, innocently picking fern fronds to use for play money. Eva," coaxed Art, "you be our dead person, and we'll bury you and give you a nice funeral. And the sand will make you feel all cool, too."

Eva said she didn't want to be either dead *or* buried, but

we promised we'd play house with her later if she'd cooperate, so finally she consented.

Scooping out a place in which Eva rather doubtfully lay down, we then began the process of packing damp sand all around her.

"Eva, quit moving," we fussed as we worked. "Lie still. You're dead."

"No, I'm not either," insisted Eva, more and more incapacitated under her heavy blanket of sand.

We worked steadily until all of Eva was covered except for her face, which stuck out as incongruously as a rose in a cowpat. We sat back on our haunches and surveyed our handiwork.

"It isn't real enough," complained Art. "You can still see her face. She can't really be dead until she's all covered."

He thought for a minute.

"I know," came that old familiar phrase, and Art was running down to the river.

He splashed over to where there were some reeds growing at the water's edge, pulled one up with a mighty heave, and returned to us.

"See this?" he asked us. "This is hollow between the joints. I'm going to fix one for Eva, and she can breathe through it while her face is covered up."

"I don't want to," whined Eva.

"It'll be fun, Eva," Art explained. "It's just like blowing bubbles through a spool remember? And it won't be but just for a minute while we pray over you."

Eva subsided. Art chose the longest joint on the stem and broke off the rest smartly. He blew through it several times to clear it, then stuck it in Eva's mouth.

"Just pretend you're blowing bubbles with a spool, Eva. Suck in, then blow out like you're making bubbles. And don't breathe through your nose."

Eva started sucking and blowing. We carefully patted sand over her face as she kept sucking and blowing. Then suddenly all that was left of Eva was a mound of sand with the reed sticking up at one end of it.

"This is perfect," commented Art. "We're ready for the funeral now."

"Art, Bert, Gerda! Come quick!"

We turned around. It was Delia who had gone to get some field flowers to decorate the grave. She was waving her arms at us frantically. "Come help me! The cows are in the wheat!"

Delia turned and ran toward the wheat-field. We jumped up and followed. By the time we had chased the wandering cows out, we had to sit down and catch our breath.

"Ugh, it's too hot for this kind of work," complained Art as he sank to rest in a shady spot.

A look of horror crossed Delia's face where she was sitting. She jumped up. "Lord-have-mercy! We forgot Eva! She's still under the sand!"

Terrified, we all jumped up and streaked for the grave, visions of a poor, smothered little girl racing through our minds. Reaching the still mound, we began throwing sand right and left in a fury of haste.

"No, no!" hollered Art. "Her face first, you dummies!" He started scraping the sand off Eva's face and we all helped. Art plucked out the reed as soon as we had uncovered her mouth, pocketing it for some future use. Immediately Eva began to howl piteously. As we worked to uncover the rest of her, we kept telling her we were sorry we took so long, but the cows got in the wheat. Finally free, Eva stood up, still sobbing. She *was* a sorry sight, with sand sticking to her everywhere — her hair, her clothes, her arms and legs.

"I'm going to tell Grandmother on you *all*," she howled. She ran off toward the house crying.

Art sat down on the pile of sand and put his chin in his hands "We never did get to have the funeral," he said disgustedly.

When we got home with the cows late that afternoon, Eva, cleaned up now, came out to meet us.

"You're all going to get a good whipping for what you did," she told us righteously.

"Who from? Grandmother or Granddaddy?" I asked. I always wanted Grandmother to be the one to punish me, as it hurt less.

"Grand*mother*!" answered Eva smartly, not realizing the relief she gave me.

"I've got an idea," said Art as we put the cows in the lot.

"What now?" asked Delia testily.

"We could get a pie pan and put it in our drawers before Mama whips us. Then we won't feel it at all."

Delia gave her brother a withering look. "Of all your dumb ideas, Art, that one is the dumbest!" she retorted.

"Well, I'm going to do it," Art came back. "You can just suffer."

He ran off towards the kitchen. Long-faced that we were going to be punished, Gerda said goodbye and plodded off for her house. When we went into the parlor, Grandmother put down her mending and asked,

"Why did you children do such a fool thing as burying

Eva? And where is Art?"

"Here I am, Mama," answered Art, popping in at the door. He was holding his hands on his seat in such a way that Delia and I knew he *had* put a pie pan in his drawers.

"You first, Arthur," said Grandmother. "I think I sense your fine hand in this." She patted her apron.

Obediently, Art lay down across it. Grandmother's first blow brought forth a strange whomp.

"What in tarnation?' wondered Grandmother. Puzzled, she felt the hidden pie pan. Yanking it out, she grew really angry.

"Young man!" she stormed as Art cowed. "You are going to get *two* spankings, one for trying to fool your elders and one for the other mischief."

And he did.

There was a drought near the end of June, and our cows now foraged farther from home each day, seeking greenery. We had long ago reached the confluence, as our grandparents called it, where Big Blue Creek flowed into the Dan. Obediently we followed as the cows picked their way steadily upstream. Then one day, as we lazily explored the new woods along the creek bank, Delia pointed out a little island in the stream, and, beyond its point, another creek, smaller and swifter. This must be the place where Little Blue Creek ran into Big Blue.

"Let's cross over and explore up the new creek," suggested Art.

The heat was awful that day, and it seemed like a cool thing to do, so we girls took off our dresses and Art his pants and, clad only in the underdrawers that Grandmother made for us out of bleached flour sacks, we forded the stream. Reaching the spit of the little island, we hurried to get our first look at the unknown territory beyond.

We had gone just a little way up the creek when we came to a place where the water spread out thinly over a wide sheet of rock, except for one place in mid-channel. There the water raced through very swiftly, boiling and churning.

Ranging on ahead as usual, Art was trying to find dry footing on the rock sheet when his foot slipped. In a flash he was caught up in the current of the cleft and shooting downstream at unbelievable speed. Because the channel was shallow, his head never did go under, but bobbed neatly along on the surface, riding like a cork. Then the water dumped him into a wide pool at the bottom of the flume and left him there.

Art stood up with a big smile on his face.

"Hey, girls!" he called out from below us. "That was the best ride I ever had! You've got to try it!"

Unconvinced, we watched as he returned and splashed back out to the place where he had slipped.

"Come on, don't be afraid! It's fun! Watch me!"

This time Art eased himself over to where the rapids began. Again the current caught him up, and again he shot downstream, racing through the froth to plunge once more into the pool.

"It does look like fun," Delia conceded.

She too eased herself over to the beginning of the sluice and bobbed off downstream. Then I tried it — it was wonderfully scary — and finally Gerda and Eva. We stayed for at least an hour, shooting the chute, as we started calling it.

Art, Eva, Delia, and I had stopped to sun ourselves on

some big rocks nearby and were sitting there idly watching Gerda, who was in hog-heaven, squealing with excitement, as she rode the waters again and again. For about the fiftieth time, Gerda edged herself over and pushed off.

Just then Art grabbed my arm and cried out, "Look!"

We looked and there, right behind Gerda as she sped merrily along, was a big black snake shooting downstream with her at exactly the same speed. There was no way to warn her — it was happening too fast. Besides, she couldn't have heard us — the water made too much noise.

So we just stood up and watched as the two of them rushed on together. Halfway through the chute, obeying some strange law of physics, the snake began to gain on Gerda and suddenly was up even with her. She may have glimpsed it then, out of the corner of one eye, for just as the water plunged her and the snake as one into the pool, Gerda began to scream mightily. The second her feet hit the bottom she was up and screeching, floundering through the water to land. The snake, probably more frightened than she, swam gracefully off downstream.

All of us were terrified of snakes, and in a body we took off running, heading helter-skelter for the friendly banks of the Big Blue, vowing never to return to that snaky place again.

In a day or two, however, with the heat continuing, and buoyed by the presence of Uncles Warren and Wright, who were already familiar with this marvel of nature (as was, we found out, practically everyone else in the countryside) we did go back. We saw no more snakes and visited the place so frequently thereafter that Grandmother took to tucking changes of underdrawers in the lard pail that contained our lunch of fried meat-and-jelly biscuits.

Chapter V

WHEELS

It was amazing how many exotic things rolled into our lives on wheels that summer. The first we knew of the gypsies was when Art came flying into the house just after the noon meal one day (letting the screen door slam behind him, which wasn't allowed) crying out, "Gypsies in town! Gypsies in town! Everybody lock up all your valuables!"

Grandmother came out into the hall with a drying cloth and a cup still in her hands.

"Hush, Arthur!" she said, frowning. "What a fuss you're making. Remember the Commandment that says we are not to bear false witness against our neighbor?"

"But Mama, Cousin Wint said Uncle Rupert has hired extra help in the store to keep them from stealing everything.

He says you have to watch gypsies like hawks 'cause they're slicker than wet rocks. They'll ask for sugar and coffee, then while you're getting that, they help themselves to a dozen other things behind your back."

"Arthur!" warned Grandmother.

Granddaddy stepped out into the hall replacing his galluses in preparation for the afternoon's work.

"What's all this about gypsies, young man?" he demanded.

"They're in Pine Hill right now, Papa, a whole caravan of them. I saw them with my own eyes, a whole field full camped over by the Dan. They travel the countryside in these wagons that have windows and doors and even a tee-tiny chimney sticking out the top, just like real houses, except on wheels."

"Arthur, calm yourself," ordered Granddaddy, "I have an acquaintance with these people. It is their habit to come through these parts every few years. There's no reason to get so up in the air about it."

"May we go see them, Grandmother?" asked Eva, who was listening with interest.

"I should say not!" replied Grandmother, turning to go back into the kitchen. "Delia, you and Bert come help me finish these dishes. Arthur, go help your Papa."

The subject of gypsies was closed and no matter how many questions we brought up over the dishes, we could get no further information from Grandmother.

All of us children were supposed to lie down for awhile in the hot part of the day, but Delia, Eva, and I usually connived to slip outside as soon as quiet signalled that our elders were busy in another part of the house. We had a rule that no one spoke until we got to the Cedar Row where we finally felt safe about escaping our naps and could talk out loud.

As soon as we got there that day, I asked Delia what she knew about the gypsies.

"They were here once when I was little. I think they camped near here, but I don't remember much about it," replied Delia with a dreadful frown that showed she was racking her brains for memories. "I can just vaguely see it in my mind's eye."

Delia put her hands to her forehead like she had a splitting headache. "I've got it! The meadow next to the road! That's where they camped. I think Warren took me on horseback to see them. But I can't recollect another thing about it. I guess I was too little." She groaned with disgust at herself.

"Why don't we go see if they're there again?" Eva wanted to know, making surprisingly good sense, and we set off down the road between the cedars. Off to one side the creek meandered in that direction, so we deserted the hot rocks of the road for the coolness of stones over which water was bubbling. It was fun balancing from rock to rock, ducking under blackberry brambles that drooped from high banks, and snatching at hovering "snake-doctors," our name for dragonflies.

We had almost forgotten our original mission when suddenly we spied — just as Art had described it — in Granddaddy's meadow — a barrel-shaped wagon painted green, with yellow-shuttered windows, a yellow door, and a little tin smokestack sticking up out of the top! Every available inch was decorated with wondrous scallops and curlicues of gilt. Even the undercarriage and wheels were gilded and striped.

A short distance away was a structure even more unusual. (We were, after all, fairly used to seeing wagons, though

43

not so wonderfully decorated ones as that.) This was a tent, shaped and colored like the cap of a mushroom. Billowing as it was in the breeze, it looked as if at any minute it might spring into the air and sail away. We could see that one side was open to the out-of-doors. The three of us stood and stared open-mouthed.

"It's them!" whispered Eva with awe. "It's the gypsies!"

"Shush!" I ordered in a low voice. "Everybody be quiet. I need to think."

As one, we crouched right down in the water beneath an overhanging bank. I tried to gather my thoughts. Curiosity was urging me forward, but somewhere in the back of my mind I recalled vague warnings about gypsies. Were they the ones who stole children? No, that was the fairies, I decided. Curiosity won out.

"I think we ought to go welcome them to Pine Hill," I announced to my companions. "It's the Christian thing to do," I added.

"Well," said Delia doubtfully.

"Grandmother will skin us alive," intoned Eva, but her eyes were shining with excitement. I knew she couldn't resist.

"Let's go then," I said, urging my little band on. The three of us stood up together and struggled up the red clay of the creek bank. A bit cautiously, we walked towards the gypsy camp over clumps of meadow grass. In front of the tent opening we could see a small fire and a kettle hanging over it. A little away from the wagon a handsome horse was grazing and flicking his tail grandly at summer flies.

Coming closer, we spied a man sitting in the shade cast

by the wagon. Next to him was a large pile of what looked like willow shoots, and he was skillfully weaving these in and out to form a basket. He looked up and saw us.

"Aha, *gorgios*!" he said, nodding, but never stopping the quick movement of his fingers. "You come to see baskets, eh?" With a smile he held a finished one out for our inspection, but we were too timid to take it. The gypsy, who had large dark eyes and a long dark curl lying on his forehead, kept on weaving for a minute, then spoke again.

"I am Jacob. You perhaps are of the Wilsons'?" (He made it sound like Wheelson). We were so quiet that he looked up to see if we were still there. I remembered my manners.

"Yes, we are Wilsons," I answered. "This is Delia, this is Eva, I am Alberta Victoria. This is my Grandfather Wilson's meadow here where you are camping."

"Aha! That I well know. We camp here before. Mr. Wheelson did me a good turn then. I never forget."

"What good turn did he do?" inquired Eva, whose curiosity always won out over her fear.

"I tell you, but first you need be made welcome to my *vardo*." Here Jacob babbled a string of strange-sounding words over his shoulder, causing a woman and five barefooted children to appear out of the dark depths of the tent. The gypsy lady, who was wearing a long skirt of dark-purplish material and many gold necklaces, at once made herself busy with the kettle.

Jacob continued to weave while the gypsy children, all dark-eyed and curly-haired like their father, settled down on their haunches to stare at us. Not wanting to stare back since we had been taught that it was rude, we satisfied ourselves with darting quick glances their way every now and then.

"Now we go to join our *kumpania* on the Dan. Last time we here my Maria very sick," Jacob told us. "Mr. Wheelson bring doctor who say Maria have the typhoid. The fever, it very bad, very high."

Now the gypsy lady handed the three of us mugs of a hot liquid which we sipped gingerly and found to be tea.

"Did Maria die?" asked Eva tactlessly.

"Aha! How can that be when that is Maria there?" Jacob answered, pointing to the tallest girl. "No, Maria live, thanks be to Mr. Wheelson. He bring ice from his ice house and we give to Maria, bit by bit, to cool her fever. And after, when the fever go, he bring the soup from Mrs. Wheelson. And Maria live, get well. I never forget."

We were feeling more at ease now and found ourselves sitting on the grass in a semicircle before Jacob rather enjoying our grownup tea, even if it was bitter. The gypsy children, somewhat raggedy in dress, had crept closer and found places on the ground near us. Jacob's work went on.

"You think you like to join with us, live Romany life?" he asked with a sly smile.

"No, thank you," I replied, wary that this might be some kind of trick to kidnap us after all.

"What is gypsy life like?" asked Eva as if she were seriously considering taking it up.

"Aha! We Romanies live fine life in open air, always traveling, seeing the new thing, never staying in one place long. Get tired of it — phwtt! Pack up tent and roll away, see new place. Food for the picking, all around; water for the drinking and washing, all around; makings for the baskets, all around. Good life. Stars, clouds overhead instead of roof. You like."

"It sounds wonderful," agreed Eva, convinced.

"Aha! We take littlest Wheelson with us then?" laughed Jacob.

"No," screeched Delia and I in horror, snatching Eva to us.

Jacob laughed and laughed. His wife, who had been plucking a chicken at the tent opening jabbered in that strange language to her husband.

"My woman say perhaps you like the *dukkering*."

We looked blankly at him. Jacob explained. "The fortune-telling, that is what we call it. Most *gorgios* like the *dukkering*. My woman says she give you your fortunes free because of Maria. You like to know the future?"

We had had our fortunes told at the school Halloween carnival by ladies dressed up like gypsies, but having our fortune told by a real live gypsy was too good to be true.

"Oh, would she? Could she?" we breathed in unison.

"Sarilda, the *gorgios* desire fortunes!" Jacob rose and held out the basket he had been putting the finishing touches on. "This for Mrs. Wheelson. You take to her, yas? Tell her from Jacob's Maria."

We nodded, overcome with the thrill of having our fortunes told. Jacob strode off toward the horse, taking his band of children with him. Sarilda took off a red silk handkerchief looped around her neck and passed it lightly across her forehead three times. Then she pulled me inside the tent. To Delia and Eva she made a motion that meant they must stay outside.

"Sit," said Sarilda, pointing to a wooden stool. I sat. The inside of the tent was so shadowy that all I got was an impression of many feather beds piled around the sides, leaving a small space in the middle where we were. Sarilda took my right hand and, after passing her kerchief across it three times, stared at it for a long tire. I was embarrassed because my hand was dirty.

Suddenly, Sarilda's head fell to one side, her eyes rolled back until only the whites were showing, and she babbled wildly in a high singsong voice. It was so eerie that I wanted to break and run, but was too scared to do so.

"You," Sarilda pointed at me, "may go on a long journey. The future here is clouded. Yes, A cloud of something — smoke, dust conceals it." Sarilda was holding her forehead just like Delia had. Maybe Delia could take up fortune-telling, I thought.

"Yes, beware!" Sarilda said again. "And beware that you not reveal what Sarilda has foretold for you. Otherwise, good fortune slip away. Now you go."

I was dismissed. "But Mrs. Sarilda," I beseeched. "Beware of ... What is it I should beware of?"

"The danger over when the Dog Days wane," said Sarilda cryptically. "Shoo."

I was pushed out into the hot sun and Delia was pulled inside instead. I stood there in a state of utter confusion. Even if I knew the future held danger now, I still didn't know what I had to watch out for. It was much worse than being blissfully ignorant of the future. And when did the Dog Days wane? I didn't even know when they started. I was wild with all kinds of new anxieties.

In a couple of minutes Delia came out of the tent with a dazed look on her face, holding up the hand that Sarilda had read as if it were made of gold.

"You'll never guess, Bert," she informed me. "I am to

be the mother of a great leader. Maybe a President!"

"Fiddlesticks!" I responded.

"Well, I could be!" Delia said angrily. "Who said you know more than a fortune teller, anyway?"

A few minutes after that Eva emerged from the tent, lips sealed tightly, determined not to lose her good fortune by talking about it. We murmured a thanks to Sarilda, who went back to plucking her chicken. We took up the gift basket and departed, no longer the carefree group we had been on the way there. I felt laden down with all kinds of new worries. What if the Dog Days didn't wane for months? Was I doomed to wait that long for some unpleasant fate? And Delia was a changed person. She gave notice that it was not dignified for the mother of a future President to be wading in creeks, and insisted on our going home by way of the road, which was ten times hotter. Eva acted as if she had been struck dumb; we hadn't heard a peep out of her since she came out of that tent.

As soon as we got to the yard, Art popped up, eaten with curiosity to know where we had been. He always sensed when we had gotten away with anything and tried to get us in trouble anyway.

"Well, if it isn't Delia and Bert and Eva coming up in the yard. Where have you all been, I wonder?" he announced deafeningly so that Grandmother would hear and take note. Delia couldn't contain herself another minute anyway and burst out with "Art, you'll never guess. We went to see the gypsies and got our fortunes told!"

"Wha-a-at?" questioned Art, unconvinced.

"And," said Delia, full of self-importance, "I am to be the mother of the President of the United States!"

Art stared blankly at his sister for a second, then exploded into guffaws. He laughed so long and hard that he fell down and rolled on the ground, completely overcome with hilarity.

"What's so funny, I'd like to know?" demanded Delia fiercely.

"You, the mother of a President," Art managed to choke out.

"Oh, Delia, why did you tell?" wailed Eva. "The gypsy lady said if you told your fortune, your good luck would slip away."

"Oh!" Delia was stricken now that she remembered. She gave Art a withering look,.

"You know what, Art? I have a good notion to grow up and run for President myself just to show you."

Art recovered and jumped up. "Mama, " he yelled so loud that you could have heard him in the next county, "these girls slipped off and went to the gypsies!"

"We were going to tell her ourselves," I told Art, " 'cause we brought Grandmother a gift from them."

I held up the basket. Until then it hadn't occurred to me how incriminating it would be. We hadn't gotten away with anything after all. Grandmother and our aunts came out on the porch to listen to all we had to report about our visit to the gypsy camp. But even the handsome basket didn't keep Grandmother from being very displeased.

. "Girls, I am extremely upset with you," Grandmother told us sternly. "You might not have been so welcome if the gypsies had not had reason to be grateful." That was as close as she would come to doubting gypsy goodwill.

When Granddaddy came in from the fields and was told, he sent us straight up to bed without supper. He wanted to give us a whipping, but Grandmother persuaded him that our going without supper would be punishment enough. Of course, we had to come down later for vespers and suffer Art's sniggering behind his hand at us.

Granddaddy's prayer that night was for the heathen in our midst. I thought for a minute he meant Delia, Eva, and me until it dawned on me he meant the gypsies. Were they heathens? I supposed they didn't have much time for church-going if they were always traveling around.

Granddaddy prayed, "Lord, work in your mysterious ways and move the hearts of the heathen to seek your kingdom. Amen."

That was the end of the gypsy episode except for one thing. In the days that followed Aunt Sadie fretted she couldn't find her favorite bantam hen anywhere, the one with the pretty-colored feathers. I didn't have the heart to tell her I saw a suspicious-looking pile of familiar feathers down at the gypsy camp.

Chapter VI

DOG DAYS

Although our days at our grandparents' were full, we never stopped wishing things could be as they were before Mama passed away. We wished we could go home. We wondered about our absent brother, Baby Clay. Papa went to see him every other week and reported that he was thriving, but we wanted to see him. Bedtime was the worst part of the day, for it was then, when we were tired, that we missed our mama most, remembering how she used to listen to our prayers every night and tuck us in with a hug and a kiss. For awhile Val and Alex would creep in from the boys' dormitory and curl up on the foot of our bed until sleep overtook them, and one of our uncles came to fetch them back.

During those first weeks the four of us were continually asking Grandmother when Papa was going to take us back home, but we never received anything more definite than a soothing mumble. However, Papa always came for Sunday dinner, and afterwards would interview us in the parlor about all our activities.

One Sunday in June Papa shocked us by saying that he had closed the house. He had built himself a slab shanty on wheels, he said, where he lived during the work week. When he wanted to go from one sawmill to the other, it was easy to have it pulled there by mules.

Val and Alex were so taken by the idea of the shanty on wheels that Papa finally gave in and let them visit him at the sawmill where it was. They came back full of all they had seen — the smart snakin' horse that eased the logs out of the fallen tree laps, the strong mules that pulled the logs out of the woods, the sawmill men with their canthooks rolling the huge logs into place to be sawn, and the circular saw that sang dangerously as it cut the wood into boards.

When Val asked him about our going home, Papa said he would be very busy all summer at the mills; maybe in the fall. Eva and I started ending our prayers with "And please, Lord, let Papa get our family back together."

In July, Granddaddy's big kitchen calendar told us that Dog Days had begun.

Naturally I immediately began to worry about the gypsy warning. We asked Aunt Sadie if this meant dogs were likely to go mad with the heat then, but she said all it meant was that Sirius, the Dog Star, would seem to rise in the sky at the same time as the sun.

"I know one thing," declared Art. "Snakes are blind during Dog Days. They'll strike at anything that moves!"

"Grandmother says you can get dew poisoning in Dog

Days if you have just one little itty-bitty sore on your toe," said Eva.

"Granddaddy said he had to get his potatoes dug before Dog Days or they would rot," I put in.

"Those are just superstitions," declared Delia.

"Delia, you wouldn't know the truth if it jumped up and bit you," remarked Art.

All I knew was that I had to be careful now that it was Dog Days. Of course, I didn't know *what of*, but soon I was so busy that I didn't have time to worry much about it.

On one of the first days of July we were surprised to look up from our play and see Granddaddy Wilson wading out into the upper wheat field. The wheat was now the toasted-cream color of Grandmother's custard pies. We ran to the edge of the field and watched wonderingly as Granddaddy broke off some wheat heads, rubbed the kernels free, and put them into his mouth where he bit down on them thoughtfully.

"Why are you eating the wheat, Granddaddy?" called Eva bravely.

"To see if it's good and dry" he answered, wading back out.

"What if it's good and dry?" Eva wanted to know.

"Then it's thrashing time," replied Granddaddy laconically as he started up the path towards the house.

The next day Granddaddy and our uncles started cutting and binding what we had guarded from the cows for so long. The wheat had demanded so much from us these past weeks that it seemed strange now to see it fall meekly before the scythe, leaving only a tame stubble behind.

In the late afternoon of the third day the shocks were carried to the barn in wagonloads and stored in the loft safe from any rain. (There had been none in a month).

Granddaddy announced at supper that he had sent for the "thrashers," and they would arrive next week. Grandmother allowed as how that would give her barely enough time to get ready. After supper, as she started outlining the work that had to be done in preparation for the big day, Eva, Delia, and I sighed inwardly. We had looked forward to some time off now that our cow-minding days were over, but it seemed we were going to be busier than ever.

✦ ✦ ✦ ✦ ✦ ✦ ✦ ✦ ✦ ✦

On the morning of the wheat-threshing, Granddaddy and the boys were up before dawn getting their regular chores taken care of before the threshing men and their machines arrived. Art was going to help Uncle Whit be the water boy, and he had bragged about it so continuously that we finally told him to shut up and quit acting so biggety. Delia, Eva, and I did the breakfast dishes, freeing Grandmother and our aunts for the preparation of the big noon meal to come.

Aunt Sadie went out in the back yard and wrung about a dozen chickens' necks. I don't know how she did it; it made me sick to my stomach! Then she and Aunt Molly and Aunt Martha scalded the feathers with teakettles of boiling water and plucked the chickens clean. It wasn't long before they had them cut up and stewing in the great pot that swung over the hearth fire.

The day before, we had peeled and cut up about a bushel of apples, and the slices had been soaking in salt water all night. Now Delia and I drained off the water and watched with admiration as Grandmother finished up her pie dough and quickly made up several big pans of apple cobbler.

Our aunts were busy snapping beans, and Grandmother was already making more pastry for the chicken pies when Mrs. Varner and Mrs. Simmons, neighbor ladies, arrived to help out.

Their husbands had brought them by the house and gone on down to the barn to give a hand forking the shocks out of the loft. We could hear the sound of the steam engine coughing as it tried to start up, and we were longing to see what was going on. Besides, the heat in the kitchen was awful, what with Grandmother cooking on the wood stove and in the fireplace as well. At last Grandmother said they could manage without us, to run along now, but be back at the sound of the dinner bell so that we could help serve. Freed at last, we raced down the path to the barn.

In the barnyard the steam engine was now throbbing steadily. Uncle Wright and Uncle Warren were bringing wood from the woodpile near the barn and heaping it on the ground close by. Art was acting like royalty, sitting high-up on the water wagon. His job (and Uncle Whit's) was to supply water from the creek to the steam engine's tank. We could see that a long belt connected the steam engine to the threshing machine.

Mr. Shopes, in charge of the whole operation, was adjusting some gears. He had a man waiting to cut the bands on the bundles of wheat and one man to feed the wheat into the thresher.

Now, seemingly satisfied that all was running smoothly, Mr. Shopes gave three long blasts on his steam whistle and signalled that the threshing was to begin. The first of the wheat was carefully guided in. Suddenly, gold grain was pouring out of a spout into a container. Uncle Warren was standing by to empty the grain into tow sacks, and helpers carried the sacks to the wheat crib. One of Mr. Shopes' men was beginning the strawstack. Granddaddy had erected poles the day before, and the stacks would be built up around these. We watched, fascinated, as straw belched out the end of a moveable pipe. Before too long, there was a nice mound of it, and the man had Uncle Wright walk on top to pack it down tight. The dust, the noise, the activity were constant, and the threshing machine seemed to us like some magical three-headed beast spouting grain, straw, and chaff in three directions at once. The steam engine poured forth an important cloud of smoke that rose in the sky and mingled with thunderheads piling up overhead.

When the dinner bell rang, the strawstacks were growing into yellow mountains, and the sacks in the granary were accumulating nicely. Remembering that Grandmother needed us, we ran back to the house.

We helped our aunts serve two table sittings. Delia passed hot biscuits, I refilled water glasses, and Eva shooed away flies. Then we got to eat some of the good food before helping clear up. As we finished the dishes, we heard a roll of thunder far off.

"God must be moving his barrels of wheat," joked Grandmother. A minute later she worried, "Oh, I do hope they finish the threshing before it storms."

We girls were sent back to the barnyard with drinking water for the men. When we got there, Granddaddy Wilson was forecasting that the dark cloud we saw building in the west would blow on over. This seemed to satisfy the men, and, after a dipper of water from our milk can, they went on with their work. The thunder kept up a rumble all afternoon, but the storm kept skirting around us.

Late in the afternoon, however, with the work just about finished, the sun was suddenly covered by a towering thunderhead with a mean-looking black bottom out of which lightning poked now and then. This gave our eyes a welcome rest from the glare, but then a hot breeze sprang up and blew dust and chaff up our noses.

Granddaddy took a look at the sky and decided this cloud meant business. He ordered the workday ended, and the two machines ground down at last and were blessedly silent. Men scurried about in the rising wind to put away equipment. Mr. Shopes tallied up how much he was owed for the job. The barnyard was almost dark now, the wind so strong you could lean against it, the animals acting skittish.

Delia, Eva, and I decided we had seen all there was to see, so we picked up the milk can and ran for the house. Lightning flashed between cloud and ground, and struck just beyond the next field. The thunder was immediate and deafening. The first cold drops of rain splashed on us, but it felt good on our sunburnt skin. Eva stuck out her tongue and tried to catch a raindrop on it as she ran. Delia and I were hurrying along, worrying that we would be struck by lightning and electrocuted by the milk can we were lugging between us. Silly and scared at the same time, we reached the house just as the rain let loose. We were glad that down at the barn the men had good shelter and time now to rest and talk over their day's work.

If we had thought we were going to get a rest now that

the wheat was harvested and off our hands, it turned out that we were wrong. Granddaddy's money crop — tobacco — needed attention next. One hot late-July morning, Granddaddy came back from the fields and announced in a voice like doom that there were too many women and children "idling" around the house. They were to get out and help with the tobacco.

It seemed the tobacco needed its first priming. This was simply pulling off the bottom leaves, the ones that had started to turn yellow. But we children were not allowed to do such important work as that. Our job came after the tobacco leaves were brought on mule-drawn sleds to the shade of a nearby tree. Working at tables made from boards and sawbucks, we were supposed to hand the leaves to the stringers. Uncle Whit, Uncle Wright, and Uncle Warren were Granddaddy's stringers, and they worked very carefully, as one loose leaf during the curing could set a whole tobacco barn on fire. With twine, they tied two or three tobacco leaves into hands. Then they tied about twenty hands onto sticks called stringer poles. At the end of the operation the stringer poles were hung in the barn on tiers that went all the way up to the very top of the building.

After a day or two, the firing took place. To cure the tobacco for market, the leaves had to be dried at high temperature. In the evenings our uncles would start fires in the brick furnaces built into the walls of the curing barns, and they would stay close by all night to keep the fires burning steadily. This was very important, as a sudden rise in temperature could scald the leaves. And when the temperature was run up to the boiling point to 'kill" the veins and stems, they had to take extra care because barns would sometimes catch fire.

All during August the primings, stringings, and firings were going on. At the time of each firing, Delia, Eva, and I begged to spend the night at the barn with the other young folks of the family. All our uncles would sleep there, taking turns checking fires and thermometers. Even our aunts occasionally spent the night, and we would hear them laughing and talking the next day about stewing chicken in a pot or roasting corn and potatoes in the coals to eat. But Granddaddy Wilson kept saying no to us. He insisted we'd be a distraction and the boys would forget to mind the temperature.

In mid-August, when we heard that one of the last big firings was to take place the next evening, we appealed to Grandmother alone. (This worked occasionally when Granddaddy was being especially strict.) We were overjoyed when she decided we might go this time if we agreed to mind Aunt Molly and Aunt Martha.

The next morning after breakfast we began elaborate preparations for our outing. We decided not to let Art in on our secrets because he had been so uppity lately. First, we told Aunt Sadie that we'd take care of feeding the chickens and gathering the eggs for her that day. When we collected the eggs, we held back half-a-dozen and hid them in the hedgerow.

Back in the kitchen, Grandmother was puzzled at the sudden drop in egg production.

"Now what can be ailing those hens?" she wondered. "I've been getting over a dozen eggs every morning this summer. Are you children sure you checked all the nests?"

"Yes'm," we nodded.

"Maybe it's dog days, Mama," suggested Delia brightly.

"Dog days?" puzzled Grandmother. "I don't follow you, Delia."

"Maybe hens don't lay good in dog days," said Delia.

"Well, I never heard that one before," replied Grandmother, turning back to her work. We had to run outside and giggle awhile in the shrubbery.

Next we went down to the creek bottom where Granddaddy had his melon patch and picked out the biggest watermelon we could find. It took a lot of effort to get that heavy melon up to the top of the hill, but pushing, rolling, tugging, and carrying in turn, we finally made it. We put the melon in a clump of high weeds beside the path.

"Now for our bedding," said Delia. We went back to the house where we succeeded in sneaking upstairs when no one was looking and slipping the quilts off our beds. Not for us those old scraps others talked about sleeping on! We were going to have the finest of beds on our outing. We hid our quilts in the boxwoods.

By late afternoon we were in a dither. We kept asking our aunts if they were ready to start for the tobacco barn yet, and they kept finding things to do, saying we would go directly. Finally their work was done, and telling Grandmother goodbye, (and trying to stay out of Granddaddy's path in case he should forbid us) we struck out. The sun was melting slowly into a puddle of hot red as we took the wagon road that led to the tobacco barn.

We had forgotten our quilts, and Delia had to run back to the boxwoods for those. Our aunts, glad to be out of the house, were chattering happily and didn't remark on our bedding.

Eva had the eggs tied up in a dishrag. We had decided Art would have to help us with the heavy melon to make up for his general nastiness of late.

Although we had been around tobacco barns all our lives (Granddaddy had three), they seemed much more exciting places to us now that we were going to spend the night at one. When we arrived, Uncle Whit had the furnaces going well and was chucking in more wood. Art was there too, all tuckered out, he said, from helping haul wood for the fire all day.

"Look what Wright caught in his rabbit gum," Art said, holding up a limp rabbit.

Uncle Wright said, "Appears like we'll be having rabbit stew for our supper tonight."

We watched as he skinned the rabbit — we each got a rabbit's foot for good luck — and cut it up. With hot coals from the furnace, he made a cooking fire a way out from under the shed roof of the barn. Aunt Molly found an old iron stew pot and dragged it out. Adding water from the supply kept on hand for flare-ups, she set the meat to cook on some flat rocks heaped in the middle of the hot coals. Eva unwrapped her eggs and pushed them into the ashes. Aunt Molly had already put in some potatoes. Uncle Whit had a dozen ears of corn slip-shucked and ready to roast.

We took Art aside and told him about the giant melon we had hidden away, waiting for just the right moment of the evening, and how we were expecting him to go with us to help bring it back. As the dark settled down and the stars began to come out, we gathered around the fire to eat all these "delectables," as Art called them.

Afterwards, "Right now would be a good time to tell

you children about the Golden Arm," decided Uncle Warren, as he sat sharpening his knife on a tobacco stick. "Have you ever heard that story?"

Entranced, we listened as he told us a scary story about a man who had an arm of gold and came back from the grave to claim it when it was stolen. Then Uncle Whit told about coming home from courting one night in the buggy, and something white jumping out of the woods right at him, scaring the horse so bad that it ran away with him and almost wrecked the buggy. Then Aunt Martha told about the time she and some of her school chums were walking by the graveyard one moonlit night, and they saw a white figure floating in and out amongst the gravestones and heard it making a weird wooing sound.

Eva's eyes were getting bigger and bigger. Even Delia and I were beginning to cast uneasy looks over our shoulders at the places where the ink of the shadows met the flickering light from the fire.

"Say, I thought you girls were going to surprise everyone with that watermelon," whispered Art as Aunt Martha launched into another story, this one about a black cat that could turn into a witch. "We'd better go before it gets any later."

"Oh, it's already too late, Art," decided Delia, looking out beyond the firelight to the black woods.

"There's a full moon rising," insisted Art, "and we'll be able to see by it. Besides, I'm craving a good piece of watermelon."

"All right!" snapped Delia crossly. "Just keep your shirt on. Wait until everybody's busy doing something, and then we'll sneak away."

We waited until our uncles went to check the thermometer in the barn and our aunts to see about some bedding, then slipped off down the path that skirted the tobacco and corn fields and led to the bottom. It was dark, but Art was right — a moon was rising and casting enough light to show us the way. We walked in silence, listening to the sound of hundreds of crickets chirping away. The ghost stories we had heard had made us edgy, and the sudden flutter of a night owl from one low limb to another caused us girls to cry out in fright. We stood there in the path, the three of us, holding on to one another.

"Oh, my heart," quavered Delia weakly. "It practically jumped out of my throat!"

"That was just an old owl," snorted Art in disgust. "Are you girls going to let some old ghost tales scare you? There's no such thing as ghosts."

"Yes, there is, too, Art," whispered Eva. "And don't say that. They might hear you and come to haunt you."

"Pish-tosh!" replied Art.

We were impressed with his nonchalance. Continuing on our way, we were able to locate the watermelon in its clump of weeds without too much trouble.

"Say, this *is* a prizewinner," praised Art, hoisting the huge melon to his stomach to get a good look. "This is one of the biggest Papa ever raised. We'll have ourselves a time finishing this one off."

With a grunt, Art heaved the melon up to his shoulder. "This thing is really heavy," he complained to us. "Must weigh fifty pounds or more."

With the memory of the ghost stories still fresh in our minds, we girls were anxious to get out of dark woods and back to the safety of the barn, so we trotted quickly off down the path. But a crackling in the underbrush close by stopped us.

"What was that?" I wanted to know.

"Nothing, of course," replied Art, pausing in the path ahead of us. "Come on, cowards."

"Wait, Art," said Delia . "I know I heard something in that dark patch over there."

Listening, we heard it again — in the dark spot right beside the path, nearer to us than we had realized — a low rustling that kept on building until it was a loud crackling that paralyzed us. Our eyes were riveted on the shadowy spot where the sound was coming from. Then, astoundingly, we saw a terrifying white face rise up out of the blackness. It gave a long, low moan. For one short second we froze where we were; then we lit off down the path, screaming for all we were worth. Art pitched the melon about a foot in the air, and we heard it hit the ground behind us and split. Art passed us running as hard as he could go.

When we reached the barn, Eva was crying and the rest of us, out of breath, were barely able to describe what we had seen.

Uncle Wright and Uncle Whit took a firebrand and went off into the dark. When they returned, they were dying laughing.

"That ghost was just one of your white-faced cows with her horns in a brushpile," Uncle Whit chortled. "Looks like you would have known her, much as you tended her this summer."

"Shucks, I knew that!" claimed Art.

"Art, you did not!" retorted Delia. "You were scareder

than *all* of us! You passed us running."

"There's some mighty fine watermelon busted up down there," teased Uncle Whit. "Anybody want to go rescue some of it?"

Eva's crying subsided into snubs, and holding the hands of our uncles for courage, we proceeded back to the scene of the 'haunting" where we salvaged enough watermelon to satisfy our cravings for a good long time.

Later, our fears laid to rest, we lay bedded down on our quilts under the shed roof, looking up at the night sky. The moon, so big at first, had climbed higher and shrunk to the size of a silver dollar. Delia was pointing out the different constellations she knew.

"Look there! Did you see that?" asked Eva. "It was a falling star."

"If you see a falling star, it means someone has died," supplied Delia.

We all lay quiet, thinking back to that cold April day when our Mama had left us.

"I thought it meant somebody is *going* to die," remarked Art from his pile of old quilt scraps. There was a long silence as we searched the sky once more. Then I was surprised by Eva, creeping up under my arm.

"Bert, that star falling? That couldn't mean Papa will die, could it?"

"No, Eva, no. Papa will be at Sunday dinner just like always, don't you worry."

We slept the night away, safe in the care of our aunts and uncles.

Chapter VII

MORE WHEELS

"I still don't see why we can't go," whined Val for about the hundredth time that week.

"*Couldn't* go," corrected Delia. "It was over last night, Val."

We were looking for blackberries down an old logging road. It was early morning and still misty in some places, giving the woods an eerie look. We were getting an early start so as to be back home before the heat of the day set in. "Well, I still don't see why we couldn't," Val said grumpily.

The topic of conversation all week had been the appearance of Colonel Jack Samson's Ranch Riders of the Old West Show in Pine Hill and the fact that Granddaddy wouldn't let any of us go. He said it was plain tomfoolery, and he didn't want to hear it even mentioned. This hurt all the more because about everyone else in Pine Hill had planned to go.

"Papa would have taken us if he had been here," said Eva sadly.

"Papa couldn't help it if he had to be in Virginia on business," I said.

"I bet it wasn't any good anyway," put in Art. "Everybody knows they are just copying Buffalo Bill and Annie Oakley's Wild West show. Probably it was boring."

Far off through the mist we heard the train whistle before it crossed the trestle over the Dan. We couldn't see it from where we were, but we knew we were very near the place where Pilgrim Church Road crossed the train tracks.

We walked on through head-high stands of pigweed, enviously picturing all our uncles, aunts, and cousins enjoying the Wild West show. Afterwards we remembered the utter stillness. Even the birds were quiet.

Then it came — the most horrendous crash of our lives!

"What in the world was that?" asked Delia, frozen in one place.

"It sounded like the train hit something," Art declared. "Come on, let's go see!"

He took off through the woods in the direction of the tracks, and we followed as fast as we could go.

What a sight — both strange and terrible — met our eyes. The train had cleared the trestle, but just beyond it had evidently smashed into another train from the opposite direction! Box cars were piled up on top of one another all topsy-turvy as if some giant had been playing blocks.

Their contents were spilled out in a motley mountain of splintered wood and bent metal. The cars not in the pile lay completely off the tracks, on their sides in a ditch. But what was truly awful was the sight of the dead and dying horses and mules strewn everywhere. Injured animals were hobbling or galloping around, whinnying with pain and fright. We saw what we knew from our schoolbooks must be buffalo wandering in a dazed way through the wreckage. Through it all swirled a cloud of mingled smoke, dust, and mist.

"Jumping Jehosophat!" hollered Art pointing to a big sign on the side of one of the boxcars. "It's the Wild West Show!"

The sign read, "Colonel Jack Samson and the Ranch Riders of the Old West."

As if at a signal, men began to climb out the windows of the overturned coaches. Some were bloody; all seemed stunned.

"We have to get help!" yelled Delia over the rising sounds of confusion. "Art, stay here and see what you can do! Bert and I will go get Papa and the boys."

Delia and I raced like madwomen through the woods, taking every shortcut we could think of. Arriving at the house, we ran in, hollering like crazy, "Help! Help! It's a wreck, a terrible wreck!"

Grandmother and Aunt Sadie hurried from the kitchen with perplexed looks. When we told all that we had seen at the train crossing, they got busy. Grandmother told Aunt Sadie to start tearing up bed sheets for bandages. She sent Delia to the fields to get Granddaddy and the boys. I was to go back to the wreck and get the show people who could walk to come to the house. Granddaddy and the boys could make stretchers out of poles and blankets, she said, for those who couldn't.

I flew back through the woods. Down at the crossing, things were worse, if possible. Men from the show were going around shooting the suffering animals. Eva and Val were standing like statues, too bewildered to move. I sent them home to help Aunt Sadie.

I went over to where Art was talking to a man with a white beard.

"This is Colonel Samson," said Art rather proudly to me. "It's his show that wrecked."

"Oh, I'm so sorry," I stammered. "My grandmother wants me to bring all who are hurt and can still walk to the house. She is sending my grandfather and uncles with stretchers for those who can't make it on foot."

"I thank you from the bottom of my heart, little lady," said the Colonel, who was wearing a fringed buckskin jacket like Buffalo Bill's and a cowboy's ten-gallon hat. He gestured toward the wreck and said, "This is a sad day, is it not? Yes, a very sad day indeed. A tragedy." He looked shrunken inside his soiled Western outfit.

Some men and three ladies I had not seen before made their way unsteadily over to where I was. The ladies were crying, and some of the men had bad cuts. They were using their handkerchiefs to staunch the blood.

One of the ladies, a pretty redhead, put her hand in mine and said, "I'm Lizzie Tascombe. We are so grateful for any help."

"Yes, ma'am,' I replied. "It's this way."

I led off through the woods with my pitiable band stumbling along behind. We had to go slowly for some of them seemed in a state of shock.

As we came into the yard, we met Granddaddy and my uncles on the way down with the stretchers.

'You are all welcome," said Granddaddy to the show

people. "I pray God will swiftly attend your needs. Bert, take them to the wash house. Your grandmother has water there for cleaning the wounds, and bandages."

At the wash house Grandmother was heating water in the wash pot. Aunt Sadie was ready with the pile of torn sheeting.

"Oh, you poor things! How terrible for you!" exclaimed Grandmother, bustling about. "Just sit down anywhere and we will get to you as quickly as possible."

While Aunt Sadie and Grandmother were washing the wounds and bandaging, I found out from Delia that Uncle Whit had driven into Pine Hill for the doctor, and that Aunt Martha had gone after neighbors who might come and lend a hand or, if that wasn't possible, send food to share.

Aunt Molly came out with a pot of coffee, which she served to the grateful show people. Aunt Martha came back in the wagon with some of the neighbor ladies and, packed in around their feet, foodstuffs donated by other neighbors. The ladies and Grandmother went into the house to prepare a meal for the crowd.

"We were headed for Baltimore," Lizzie Tascombe told us as she rested on the front porch. She kept fiddling with the bandage on her arm, "Maude and I had just finished having breakfast with Colonel and Mrs. Samson in their car."

Eva, who had a talent for cutting through courtesy to get at the meat of the matter, asked, "What do you do in the Wild West show?"

"Well, honey, I guess you'd say I am their Annie Oakley. I do trick riding, sharpshooting, and rope tricks. I can shoot straight through the center of a playing card and that's while it's in midair! I was always a tomboy who could do things better than my brothers. One day my sister Maude here and I went to see Buffalo Bill's show, and we loved it! I came home and started practicing, and it wasn't long before I could do it all. Had to run away to join the show, though. My mama wouldn't hear of it. She wanted me to get married and raise a passel of babies. Ha! I hope she never hears about this wreck. If she ever does, she'll say 'I told you so,' for sure."

The third lady, we learned, was Colonel Samson's wife, Edith. She had white hair like her husband, and kind brown eyes that looked very worried. She kept saying over and over into her handkerchief, "Oh, dear! Oh, dear! I don't know what Jack will do now. This will ruin him, simply ruin him!"

About then Art arrived in the yard with more show people. He reported to us the news that about twenty horses had been crushed to death, and all but a few of the others were so badly injured they had to be shot. He said Whit, Warren, Wright, and some of the neighbor men were digging a pit to bury them in. I was glad I wasn't down there to see it. The doctor had come to the wreck, Art continued, and moved two men who were badly injured to his house in town.

"Does anybody know what caused the wreck?" asked Delia.

"They say a fast southbound freight ran into the show train head-on," answered Art, pleased to be the bearer of important news.

Granddaddy and our uncles drove up in the yard at that moment. The wagon was loaded with trunks that, no doubt, belonged to the show. A few minutes after that some men came up driving three buffalo before them. They shut the buffalo up in the pasture with our cows. I wondered if Queenie would try to boss these strange-looking newcomers.

wanted to say thank you in a special way, so, Mr. Wilson, I want you to accept one of my horses as a token of appreciation. Boys!"

Out came two men and, between them, the prettiest roan mare I had ever seen. The Colonel patted her lovingly. It was obvious she was a special pet of his. "This is Bonnie, Mr. Wilson. She's yours, now."

We saw Granddaddy rise from his chair and go forward to take the reins.

"Well. I never expected anything like this, I can tell you. What we did we were glad to do without reward. But I do thank you, Colonel Samson. She is a real beauty."

The two men shook hands. Then the show people rode off to the pasture. We all clapped and clapped until our hands hurt.

Val and Alex said they had never had such a good time before. As we walked back to the house through a night filled with stars and crickets, I suddenly remembered my gypsy fortune. Could the train wreck have been the danger I should look out for? The gypsy had said something about smoke and dust, and there had certainly been plenty of that. Could the Dog Days be waning now?

"Aunt Sadie," I asked of the figure who was walking the path directly ahead of me, "do you know when the Dog Days wane?"

Aunt Sadie shifted her lantern to her other hand and turned to look back at me in its light. "Well, Bert, the calendar says Dog Days end on the fifteenth of August, and today is the fifteenth, so I suppose they have. Why?"

"They have been very suspenseful, " I said mysteriously.

Chapter VIII

"The Goldenrod is Yellow"

The goldenrod is yellow,
The corn is turning brown,
The trees, in apple orchards
With fruit are bending down.*

It was time now for the protracted meeting at our church. Aunt Sadie was in her element. Her clothes, which she had made especially for this event, had been ready for weeks. She had a new black straw hat, and the rest of the family were suitably polished up. Eva and I had new white dresses and

*From "Poems" by Helen Hunt Jackson,
Copyright, 1892, by Roberts Brothers

new ribbons (mine blue, Eva's pink) which Papa had sent for us from Uncle Rupert's store in Pine Hill. We left for church only after Aunt Sadie had inspected us from tip to toe to make sure we were perfectly groomed and outfitted.

The first big meeting of the week lasted from eleven to one o'clock Sunday with dinner on the grounds afterwards. We were glad to see some of the kin we had been too busy to visit of late. Gerda was there with her family, and she was wearing a dress that fit, more or less, and *shoes*!

'Gerda!" we exclaimed, running up to her. "Where have you been so long?"

"Law," said Gerda in her drawl. "I've helped Mama put up everything in the garden except for the dirt!"

"Come on," we said, grabbing her by the hand. "Let's go load up on some fried chicken."

"I'll say," added Art. "There must be fifty different kinds of pie and cake here today."

The visiting preacher was a Reverend O'Dare from South Carolina. To me he seemed awfully ugly — tall, gangly, and afflicted with a huge Adam's apple that bobbed up and down with every word he spoke — but everybody agreed he preached a good sermon.

It was ferociously hot in the church when we returned for the service that night. All the ladies were batting the air with pasteboard fans depicting, in garish color, the Last Supper on one side and the Crucifixion on the other. Our clothes were sticking to the pews, and Alex kept lifting up first one leg and then the other.

"Alex, stop fidgeting," I whispered to him. "Why do you keep doing that?"

"Because," he whispered back to me, "I'm afraid if I

don't, I'll get stuck to the varnish and have to stay here forever."

Reverend O'Dare was now making an impassioned plea for all sinners to come down to the altar and be saved. We had sung every verse of "Almost Persuaded," and now the choir started "Just As I Am." It was time for those who had been persuaded to go down front and unite with the church. I sat back and observed smugly, for I had been saved the year before, and had joined the church *and* been baptized in Mill Creek. (It was October before the visiting preacher got back for the baptizing, and the water was so cold as I waded in that I was tempted for a minute to just go back to my life of sin.)

When I heard a stirring at the end of our pew, I looked around to see Eva pushing past everyone's knees. Eva was going down to the altar! Her round little face shown with perspiration, giving her a saintly look as she floated down the aisle. I knew this would please Aunt Sadie and Granddaddy no end.

Reverend O'Dare spread his fingers wide over Eva's head and prayed that her sins become as white as snow. Then, in a low voice, he asked some question to which Eva gave mumbled replies. Reverend O'Dare expressed his congratulations to Eva and then asked the congregation to rejoice in the rescue of another lost soul.

Evidently Eva's example melted some hearts, for before we sang another whole verse of "Just As I Am," three others made their way to the front. Reverend O'Dare was ecstatic.

After services everybody came up and shook Eva's hand or patted her head. Aunt Sadie put her arm around Eva and said, "You have made us all so proud and happy tonight, Eva."

Granddaddy said to her, "Young lady, I have a copy of

the New Testament at home that shall be yours!"

Eva was drinking in all this praise and attention like a plant does rain at the end of a long drought. On the way home, she told Delia, Art, and me, "You know, it was the most peculiar thing. Something seemed to just push me right out of my seat. And when I started down the aisle it was as if my feet were going along by themselves all the way to the altar."

Monday night services were hot, too. The church was not as full, but attendance was still good. We had worked in the tobacco all day, and I was hoping for a short service. After a long sermon and a lot of hymn-singing, Reverend O'Dare came to the closing part of the meeting, the call for souls to be saved. The choir sang "Just As I Am." The ladies' fans flicked busily back and forth, but nobody moved to go down to the altar even though Reverend O'Dare signalled the choir to run through "Just As I Am" again, and even threw in a few words about eternal damnation. He was standing there, his arms outstretched beseechingly to the congregation, when I heard a rustle along our pew. I was startled to see Eva push past. She was going down to the front again. As she brushed by, Aunt Sadie tried to grab her by the dress-tail, but missed.

Reverend O'Dare got a strange look on his face when he saw that the same sinner had returned to be saved. But, since he probably couldn't think what else to do, he gamely went through the whole routine again.

Eva seemed transported by it all. When a man from the back of the church joined her at the front, Reverend O'Dare seemed mighty relieved to have a fresh convert to practice on. At the end of the services, Aunt Sadie explained to Eva as gently as she could, "Honey, once you are saved, you are saved forever. You don't have to keep going down."

"I know, Aunt Sadie," replied Eva, "but I felt sorry for that poor preacher. He just kept begging and begging, and nobody would go, so I thought I'd help him out."

"It appears to me," said Granddaddy a little wryly, "that Eva has more of the Christian spirit about her than most."

✦✦✦✦✦✦✦

Muscadines (we called them muskydines) were ripening in the hot sun, and we spent whole mornings searching out the tangled vines in the woods so that Grandmother could make her wonderful, mouth-watering jelly. One morning before we left on our search, Papa appeared in the yard with his usual fall visitors, the president of the Norfolk and Western Railroad and some of his top men who always came during bird-hunting season. They stood around in their fancy shooting garb and talked with Granddaddy about how the opening of the Panama Canal was going to mean progress for the South, and how they expected the North-South railroad lines in the country to become much more important with the increased trade the canal would bring.

While the men were exclaiming over how much we had grown, Val asked if they had drunk up all of Uncle Sid's locust beer (which Papa always had made up in a barrel for their visit). Hurriedly, Papa changed the subject because Granddaddy Wilson believed strong spirits to be evil, and wine a mocker.

"Well, children," said Papa to us, "I think I have some good news for you. I passed by your Granddaddy Barrister's on the way here this morning, and he told me he was making molasses and you're invited over to help him. How would that be?"

We were glad of the invitation, for we loved going to see our Granddaddy Barrister. And how we loved it when he dipped a piece of cane down into the thickening sorghum and handed it to us to eat like a lollipop. Just thinking about the coolness of the crisp stalk blending with the warmth of the smooth syrup made us hungry for some.

The next morning Uncle Sid came in Papa's wagon to take us to our Granddaddy's. We had missed Uncle Sid more than we realized and had much to tell him of all our summer-time adventures. After a bit though, we noticed the wagon was rolling past our old home. It was the first time we had seen the place since Mama passed away, and talk in the wagon fell off as we stared. We had put all of it so thoroughly out of mind that the sight of that deserted porch — Mama's plants (the few not adopted by her sisters) withered to skeletons and rattling in a fitful breeze, the chairs turned back against the wall in an unwelcoming manner — devastated us. It seemed we should see Aunt Sally out in the back doing the laundry, or Mama bending over her vegetable patch.

Emotions long stifled rose up and I saw some tears brushed quickly away. Uncle Sid hurried the horse with a 'Giddyup!" and started to talk to us about what we were going to do at Granddaddy Barrister's.

When we arrived, we found our Grandfather occupied at his cane mill. His mule, Bandy, walked patiently round and round a worn circle, turning heavy stones which ground the cane stalks between them until sap ran down into wooden buckets. The buckets were emptied into a long shallow pan suspended over a fire which slowly boiled the juices down to molasses.

In the fall, neighbors brought their cane harvest to Granddaddy to be made into winter sweetening, and he kept a portion for his payment. Those without cane crops came also, bearing jugs and other covered containers, to buy Granddaddy's molasses.

Our Granddaddy Barrister was the very embodiment of the true Christian gentleman. I thought he looked just like Robert E. Lee. The gentlest, most soft-spoken man in creation, his acts of charity abounded. He was so well thought of in the community that he had served as superintendent of Pine Hill's Methodist (and only) Sunday School for over thirty-five years.

After his wife, our Grandmother Matisha, died, Granddaddy called his way of life "batching around the place."

"It's a hog life, children," he would say with a twinkle in his eye as he baked sweet potatoes in the coals or popped corn on a shovel for our supper.

Once, Granddaddy discovered a still hidden away on a distant corner of his land. Whereas Granddaddy Wilson would have unhesitatingly razed it, tenderhearted Granddaddy Barrister, knowing the bootlegger had a family to feed, told him to finish his run, then get the still off his property once and for all.

We spent the day at Granddaddy's helping him keep the molasses fire going. We all got to ride Bandy round and round.

Perhaps he sensed a melancholy in us because before too long he began to speak to us of our mother.

"Children, I haven't had the chance to see you since your mother departed this earth, but I've been thinking of you and praying for you. Your mother would be proud to see how well you are coming along. This is a time in your lives when religion can be a great comfort, for it is promised in that great and good Book that if we live right we will be reunited with those we love one day. You mustn't grieve too much. Your mother is in a wonderful place beyond sorrow and toil."

When we were leaving at sunset in Uncle Sid's wagon, Granddaddy said, "Next week there is to be a corn shucking at Aunt Nella and Uncle Dwight's, and she told me to invite you. I suspect that's welcome news."

And he was right about that, for corn shuckings were a looked-forward-to event every fall.

The next week Uncle Sid was sent to fetch us to Aunt Nella and Uncle Dwight's whose farm lay just on the other side of Pine Hill. We got there at dusk when the corn-shuckers were almost ready to begin. The first thing we saw was a brown mountain of pulled corn in the barnyard. Around its edge, folk of all ages were standing, talking, sitting (on low chairs or stools), running, playing, laughing, joking. At the far side of the barnyard, ladies were cooking up a huge pot of brunswick stew. Our young cousins came to greet us at once, and we took time to talk over what had happened during the summer months. Then the boys pulled Val and Alex away to see some new goats down at the barn.

Belle said to Eva and me, "Come and see what we are going to eat tonight!" She led us to the pie safe in the kitchen. Opening it, she counted out the goodies.

"There's sweet potato pie, and pumpkin pie, and dried apple pie, and persimmon pudding, and blackberry cobbler, and a walnut cake and a caramel cake! Did you ever see so many good things to eat?"

Next she took us in to see the visiting babies, three of them, lying side by side on the company bed. Two were fast asleep, while the other just lay there kicking and looking around.

Uncle Dwight's mother, who was to tend the babies for the night, said, "Hello, girls. How would you like to take one of these darlings home with you?" She was doing some crochet work to while away the time as she rocked.

We heard voices raised in excitement and hurried out to find that the shucking had begun. A lot of the men were betting they would be the first to shuck all the way through the corn pile. All the children were bunched together down at one end, and we went to join them.

Johnny Lee Whitaker, whom I knew from Sunday School, was boasting, "I'm going to kiss every girl here tonight because I'm going to find all the red ears in that pile!"

But in a minute, "I found one!" hollered Uncle Dwight from down at the other end. He held it aloft. "Here's the first red ear!"

"Go get your kiss, Dwight," hollered everybody.

"Aw, I'm too old for that foolishness," he returned, grinning, but such a big outcry went up that he had to get up and go find Aunt Nella beside the cook-pot and give her a kiss.

It wasn't long before the boys got tired of just shucking the shucks and began pitching them at one another. Then they started in on the girls, and we had to get up and run, dust down our backs and cornsilk in our hair. Johnny Lee and his friends chased Eva, Belle, and me all the way out of the barnyard into the dark where there were shadowy, mysterious places beyond the reach of the hanging oil lanterns. Giggling until it hurt, Eva and I kept stumbling up against unfamiliar objects such as chicken coops and watering troughs. We finally thought we had found a good hiding place behind the corncrib when over our heads there was a sudden squawking, and three hens came flapping down on top of us. We had disturbed their roosting place in a low tree, which sent us into more giggles.

Back in the barnyard the womenfolk had set up a long table and covered it with jars of pickles and the different desserts and dishes for the brunswick stew, so supper was announced.

After our meal there was a little more work and then, suddenly, the husking was completed. Now there were two piles in the barnyard, one of corn ears and one of shucks.

"Let's get these shucks squared away, everybody," someone yelled. Laughing, a row of people linked arms and, walking close together, kicked a wave of shucks along in front of them to the shuck-pen. Others just gathered up as many as they could carry and tried to get there without dropping any.

People were beginning to leave for home. Johnny Lee came over to where I was standing with Belle and Eva and said, "I'm still mad because I didn't get that kiss from you, Alberta, but I aim to before too long. There's more shuckings coming, you know." But just then his parents called to him from their wagon and he ran off.

Eva and I were to spend the night, and after the company had gone, all the talk in Belle's bed was of how I had caught myself a beau. And although I complained loudly, I was secretly thrilled.

Chapter IX

THE GREAT CONFLAGRATION

With the coming of fall and cool weather, Papa abandoned his heatless shanty and took a room at Uncle Henry's
house in Pine Hill. It seemed he had forgotten saying that we
might go back home when summer was over. Eva and I were
afraid to broach the subject because Grandmother had told us
that Papa wasn't over Mama's going yet, and we mustn't upset him by begging to go home.

After all the crops were in, school started. With some of
the tobacco money, Grandmother Wilson bought a bolt of un-
bleached muslin for making our petticoats and drawers, and
bolts of brown and blue gingham for making our school frocks.
When the days began to cool, she also made us start wearing

our winter underwear, which I hated as there was no way on earth to get stockings pulled up over it smoothly — they always wrinkled up — and I lived in daily mortification at the ridges running around my legs.

Papa had at last consented to let us attend public school in Pine Hill with most of our kin. My teacher, in the elementary section, was Mrs. Freda Barter, and Eva's, in the primary section, was Miss Bess Woodhouse. On one of those first walks home after school, Eva was rhapsodizing over her new teacher.

"Miss Woodhouse is the prettiest lady I know! She wears her hair up real high in the front, and every day she has a brooch pinned to her dress, and she has the nicest, kindest eyes!"

Art, tagging along behind with some boys, overheard all this and hollered to Eva, "Your teacher's an old maid!"

"She's not! She's not old! She's beautiful!" championed Eva.

"Well, she may not look so old," replied Art, "but she's an old maid, all right. And I should know 'cause Cousin Wint told me so. And he ought to know 'cause she boards at his house!"

"Art, what are you talking about?" inquired Delia, always ready to set her brother straight. Art left his friends and trotted up to join us.

"Wint said he heard his mother talking before Miss Woodhouse moved in. Aunt Tess has some friends in Boone's Rest where Miss Woodhouse comes from. Wint heard her tell his daddy that they say Miss Woodhouse is 'way over thirty years old and an old maid. Seems she has all these brothers who scare off every suitor who comes a-courtin'."

"She's not an old maid! You take it back, Art, or else!" Eva was ready to fight to defend her teacher's name, so Delia and I moved in to smooth things over.

"Eva, an old maid doesn't have to be old. It just means she hasn't got married yet, that's all," we tried to explain. But Eva was mad enough to walk ahead of us the rest of the way home.

On the day of the Great Conflagration, as the family always called it thereafter, Eva and I had walked the mile to school as usual, had completed our first two hours of lessons, and were out with the rest of the school for recess when we heard, far off in the distance, a bell clanging. Eva and I recognized the sound right away; it was Granddaddy's dinner bell. We sought out each other in alarm, for it was not noon, and we knew the bell would be rung for only one other reason — help was urgently needed!

We immediately ran inside to our teachers and begged to be allowed to go home and find out what was wrong. Sympathizing with our concern, they said we could go if we would be back within the hour. Promising to do so, we flew off down the road for home.

Once we had topped Soapstone Hill, we could see clouds of smoke rising in the air in the direction of Granddaddy's. Our home was on fire! We began crying and running at the same time. On the road, clattering wagons passed us, driven by neighbors hurrying out to help. We reached the Cedar Row with our sides aching. We could see the house now. Thank goodness, it wasn't on fire.

But behind the house down in the barnyard, we could see where the fire had already done its work, the hay and straw stacks completely burnt up, leaving only big black circles on the ground where they had been. The corn and wheat cribs were now fiery skeletons glowing their last, ready at any moment to collapse into embers.

A chain of men was passing along buckets of water from the creek, and wetting down the sides of the cow barn and stable, scorched and smoking from the nearby heat.

We spied Aunt Molly at the edge of a group of women who stood watching anxiously.

"Aunt Molly," we panted, tears of fright still on our cheeks. "What happened?"

"Your brothers have just burned up all the corn and wheat and hay for the winter, that's what happened!" she spat out at us venomously.

Shrinking from her, we looked for Val and Alex.

"Come on, Eva," I said. "We have to find them. And I think I know where they'll be."

I knew where Val's secret hiding place was because we had found it together one day last summer while looking for turkey nests. It was a rounded-out space in the hedge that grew against the back of the smokehouse where Grandmother stored her canned goods. Down at the roots of the thick bushes was a place big enough for Val and a companion, usually Alex, to sit and play. Val kept his treasures there, some shiny rocks and a few Indian arrowheads.

Eva and I skirted the crowd of milling men and worried women, and headed for the smokehouse. It was on the far side of the house, which muted the sounds of turmoil. Making ourselves as thin as possible, Eva and I slid along the narrow space between the smokehouse and hedge.

"Val, Alex," I called in a stage whisper. "Are you in there?"

I saw Val's head, then Alex's, pop sideways out of the hideout up ahead.

"Yes, we're here," answered Val.

Eva and I somehow managed to squeeze ourselves in with them in the little space remaining. Sharp roots cut into our legs; leaves and limbs poked into our faces.

"What happened?" we wanted to know. "Did you *really* burn down the stacks and cribs?"

Val then told us everything that had occurred. After we left for school that morning, he and Alex had passed through the kitchen on their way outside to play. Grandmother, Aunt Sadie, and Aunt Molly were in the parlor finishing a quilt on the quilting frame. Granddaddy, Uncle Whit, Uncle Warren, and Uncle Wright had gone to the hillside lot to cut wood for the winter.

"Alex and I saw a box of matches on the table," Val told us, wiping away the tears that wouldn't stop flowing, "and we took three. We went out to the barnyard and sat down beside the haystack. It was cold, so we decided to light a match. Alex was just sitting there holding the match to get warm when it caught on some straw right next to his foot. I thought *he* was going to catch on fire, so I raked it away from him quick. Only I guess I raked it in the wrong direction because all of a sudden there was this whoosh! and the whole side of the stack was on fire! It scared us bad. By the time we got up, the whole stack was burning. We were going to run get Granddaddy fast, so we started to crawl under the fence next to the haystack. But we got stuck in the barbed wire. Both of us. Finally, I got loose, and then I got Alex loose. But I had to tear our shirts."

Val stopped long enough to wipe his nose on his now-torn shirttail.

"We ran quick as lightning to the parlor and told Grandmother and Aunt Sadie and Aunt Molly the hay was on fire. They all said, 'Oh, my goodness!' and jumped up, and Aunt Sadie ran out back and started ringing the dinner bell for all she was worth. Then the rope broke, and she was just standing there holding the broke end. We could see from the yard that the fire had spread to the corn crib and was blazing higher. Aunt Sadie hiked up her skirt and shinnied straight up that pole, and grabbed the short end and started ringing the bell again. She was a sight to behold!" For a moment Val was lost in admiration of his aunt.

"Then Granddaddy and the boys came running out of the woods and tried to put the fire out, but by then everything was all burnt up. 'Cept for the barns, and they started throwing water on them. And then Alex and I ran away," he finished lamely.

The four of us digested all this for awhile.

"Val, Alex," I told them firmly, "you have to come out now and face your punishment. You can't stay in here and hide like cowards."

There was a long silence. Alex's eyes were big and blue and so sorrowful. I felt especially sorry for him.

"I guess you're right," said Val at last.

We all crawled out and regretfully went to find Granddaddy. The barn, the stable, and all the animals were saved, we found. The straw was not an important loss, and much of the hay was still piled safely in the fields for the animals to eat into all winter. What was gone forever was all the corn and wheat for the winter ahead. Granddaddy Wilson took Val and Alex to the smokehouse and whipped them with a brush broom. Later, Papa came from his work at the sawmills to have a talk with them.

"Boys," he began sternly when he had them alone. "I hope you realize the seriousness of what you have done."

"But Papa," explained Val in a frustrated tone. "We were just trying to get warm."

"I imagine your grandfather has warmed you up considerable by now, am I right?"

"Yes, sir," the two answered earnestly.

"Now, the three of us are going to sit down and talk about what the loss of all their corn and wheat will mean this winter to Granddaddy and Grandmother, and your aunts and uncles."

Val has always said the next half-hour was one of the most painful of his childhood.

Chapter X

CHRISTMAS GIFTS

It was on a frigid, sunless afternoon in December that I came up with my glorious idea. If it worked, Papa would see how loved Eva and I were, and be so proud of us that surely he would want us to be together again.

In the parlor Aunt Molly, Aunt Martha, Delia, and Eva were gathered around the organ as Aunt Sadie played songs for them to sing. There was now an argument going on about what song would be next. Delia wanted "Home on the Range," but Aunt Sadie reminded her that Granddaddy Wilson allowed only hymns to be sung on Sunday. And although Delia insisted that she didn't see anything sinful about "Home on the Range," Aunt Sadie refused to be swayed. Finally, they began "Shall We Gather at the River," a ridiculous choice for such a miserable day.

I punched Eva on the arm and beckoned her out to the icy hall. She followed reluctantly.

"Come on," I whispered.

"Come where? Bert, it's cold out here."

"Come on upstairs, Eva. I just got a wonderful idea!"

Mystified, Eva followed me up to our unheated bedroom where our breath-clouds hovered before us in the still cold air.

"Sh-h-h," I cautioned, tiptoeing over to the corner where there was a trunk containing all the things we had brought from home.

"What in the world are you doing?" asked Eva as I dug down into its depths with my arms.

"I told you, Eva. I am letting you in on a wonderful secret idea. I have money saved from my "Grit" route, and with it we can buy everyone in Pine Hill School a Christmas gift!"

Eva looked shocked at my announcement, but I could see her slowly getting used to the idea. I kept groping around under the clothes and finally located it, the little wooden box I called my treasure box. Inside was my "Grit" money.

"I *would* like to get Miss Woodhouse a lace handkerchief like the one Aunt Tess gave me," Eva started to muse, "and Gerda some warm mittens. And Betsy Huston that sits next to me has never had an orange. And we could get Nell Simmins a..."

"Didn't I tell you it was a wonderful idea?" I gushed, interrupting her visions. I poured all my money out and counted it up.

"Will that be enough?"

I was having doubts now about the scope of my plan. "Well, it's not as much as I thought I had," I admitted. "Anyway, you have to put in your money too. How much do you have?"

"I've got two dimes I made swatting flies for Grandmother!" answered Eva, excited now.

"That's not much. We're going to need more money than this. Wait! I have an idea! You know Papa's big black safe in the company bedroom?"

Eva nodded. Both of us knew that after Mama died, Papa had moved it to Granddaddy's. With our house closed, he felt better keeping it here, especially since each fall the sharecroppers on his land entrusted him with the money for their spring fertilizer. Like my Papa, I was born with a good head for figures, and when I was little more than a toddler, he had taught me the safe's combination and delighted in watching me whirl the dial around and, at a click, throw open the door.

"We can borrow some money from there," I said. "We'll only take a little, and then after Christmas we can work hard and make money and put it back before it's even missed. Isn't that a good idea?"

"I guess," said Eva doubtfully. She was so wishy-washy, I thought. "Anyway, you can't open that heavy safe. Papa's the only one who knows how."

"Yes, I can, too. Papa taught me how when you were still a baby. Come watch!"

We hurried to the company bedroom and stooped in front of the huge bulk of the safe. I twirled the dial a few times to warm it. Carefully, I matched up the arrow with the numbers and rotated the dial one, two, three. Then almost as if no time had elapsed since I last accomplished it, I once more swung open the door in triumph. Inside, in cigar boxes, lay neat stacks of bills held together with rubber bands. I recognized George Washington's picture on the top of one stack and took three bills from there.

"That ought to do it," I said with a feeling of great satisfaction at solving our problem. "Do you think I should put in an IOU? Papa says if you borrow money that you should always give an IOU."

"Yes, lets," replied Eva, but just then we heard footsteps on the stairs, and in a panic I slammed the safe door closed. I hid the money in my pocket with our other change and trying to look completely innocent, walked sedately out of the room.

It was only Aunt Sadie after all, but still I whispered to Eva, "Don't tell anyone anything! We'll meet after school tomorrow to go buy the gifts."

The school day crawled as we contemplated the pleasure we were going to get — and give — buying gifts that afternoon. Four o'clock came at last, and, telling Delia and Art we were to meet Papa at Uncle Rupert's store (I thought my lie a good one), we raced each other down the road to town.

I knew we didn't dare go to Uncle Rupert's store with all that money — he would say something to Papa for sure — so we went to B. R. Hodgkin's General Merchandising instead. It was the only store in town not run by our relatives. Perhaps Mr. Hodgkins would think only that, our Mama having passed away, Papa had given Eva and me the job of doing a lot of Christmas shopping.

Mr. Hodgkins nodded as Eva and I entered. His son,

B.A., came to wait on us which was good because, being young, he would be less likely to question our unaccustomed wealth. Eva and I cruised up and down the store aisles, selecting wondrous treasures.

First, Eva chose the store's laciest handkerchief for Miss Woodhouse. Next, for Nell Simmins, we got a real, honest-to-goodness jump rope to take the place of the muskydine vine length she usually turned for us. We picked out an assortment of whirligigs, little china dolls, and tiny parasols that actually opened and closed. We couldn't resist a miniature set of cast-iron cooking utensils, and lastly, we asked for a bag of stick candy, and one of oranges. I signaled to Eva that we'd best stop for the day as we had about all we could carry.

B.A. eased our purchases into two sacks, and I paid him. Fortunately, B.A.'s daddy was busy in the back and didn't note the unusual extent of our shopping.

Eva and I hurried across the rigid ruts of the road back toward the schoolhouse. We had already decided where we were going to hide our surprises. We figured nobody would willingly go to the graveyard this time of the year, so we hid our sacks in the dead weeds beside the pillared entrance. Thankfully, we got to Granddaddy's before suppertime and had to make explanations only to Delia, saying that Papa had been too busy to get away and meet us.

The next morning we arose elated at the thought of all the Christmas joy we were going to spread. At the graveyard entrance, I pretended to turn my ankle, as planned, and Eva volunteered to help me along, urging Delia, Art, and the rest of our kin to go on ahead into the warm schoolhouse. Then, when they had disappeared inside, Eva and I scurried over and extracted our sacks. We discussed the best time for distributing the gifts. I thought it would be safer to wait until school let out for the day, but eager Eva said she couldn't wait a minute past recess. So we decided to have our friends, those to be favored with gifts that day, meet us in the front cloakroom then.

Throughout the next two hours, Eva and I were whispering our summons importantly, demanding strict secrecy. Thus it was that after the rest of the children went unsuspectingly out to play, a little band of curious friends gathered around in the cloakroom. There we revealed, beneath coats artfully draped on the floor (as if they had accidentally fallen) our richly-laden sacks.

"Christmas gift!" we greeted each friend traditionally as we doled out the surprises. Our friends, at first stunned, soon were beside themselves with delight. For those of us in the cloakroom, recess seemed over in an instant; we had scarcely had time to examine, exhibit, and discuss the merits of, much less try out, the gifts when the rest of the school came trooping in, chapped and puffing from the cold outside.

Eva and I were flying high, floating blissfully on clouds of gratitude gasped out by our friends. But, in all the excitement, we had neglected to announce that we intended eventually to bring something for everyone. We had failed to reckon that those without gifts would be feeling jealous, left-out, and angry. Our happiness lasted through lunch, which naturally we spent with our grateful friends in one select corner of the auditorium (where pupils were allowed to eat in cold weather.) At the end of lunch period, I saw children talking to our teachers. Mrs. Barter and Miss Woodhouse had a whispered conference, and then Eva and I were summoned to the privacy of the hall to be questioned.

"Alberta, what is this we are hearing about you and Eva giving expensive presents to twelve friends?"

"Was it only twelve?" asked a deflated Eva. "I thought it was more than that."

"Alberta?" Mrs. Barter was waiting for my explanation.

"Yes, ma'am," I answered. "We did give Christmas presents to some of our friends this morning. And," I hurried on to add, "we are going to have gifts for the rest of our schoolmates by tomorrow."

"I have your present in my pocket, Miss Woodhouse," said a tremulous Eva. "It is so pretty and frilly it reminds me of you." And with that Eva pulled out the lace handkerchief, still pinned to tissue paper, and offered it to Miss Woodhouse. Her gesture would have melted the heart of Beelzebub.

Miss Woodhouse's stern look softened.

"Eva, dear," she said, sinking to her knees so that her face was on a level with Eva's, "wherever did you get the money for all those presents?"

Eva turned and looked expectantly at me.

"I had money from my "Grit" route and Eva had some money from swatting flies, and then I opened Papa's safe and we borrowed some of the money that was in there. We were going to work and pay it back after Christmas. I was going to put in an IOU, but we got in a hurry," I confessed, getting more and more tearful as I went along.

Abruptly I saw our generosity anew. Even though we said we were borrowing, what we did was steal! Taking someone's money that was not ours, money not even Papa's without their permission, was the same as stealing!

"Alberta, Eva, we are going to send for your father. This

is a very serious offense, and he needs to know about it."

As Eva and I waited for Papa to arrive, we were wishing we could die. It would have been easier than facing him. When he did come down the long dim hall, we almost didn't recognize him, dressed in his best suit and looking so tall and handsome. I guess he figured his work clothes would not be appropriately serious for a conference at school.

We sat down in the little office, and, after the introductions, Mrs. Barter began by explaining how some of the children had come to her at lunch and reported that we had handed out gifts to about twelve of our friends. She then described our questioning in the hall and how I said I had acquired the money. When she came to that part of the story, Papa looked stunned. He gave me such a look of disappointment and hurt that I felt like the lowest of worms.

"And Eva?" he asked. "How was she involved in this?"

"I involved her, Papa," I spoke up. "She wouldn't have done it if I hadn't coaxed her into it. It was all my fault."

"I see," said Papa. He sat very still for a moment, looking down at the floor. I could see his knuckles whiten where he was gripping the chair arm.

"Alberta, do you realize what you have done?" asked Papa at last, his eyes reaming into the very soul of me.

"Yes, Papa," I whispered.

"Speak up, Alberta."

"Yes, sir, I stole. I took money that wasn't mine. I broke one of the Commandments. But, oh, Papa," I wailed, finally breaking into sobs, "I only thought to make my schoolmates happy. I know I went about it wrong, but *that* was what I intended to do."

Then Papa's arms were holding me tight, his cheek

pressed against mine.

"Alberta, I believe you realize how wrong you were and that you're truly sorry. So what I will do is make up for the money you took from the safe and arrange a plan with your grandmother whereby you and Eva work to pay me back. Then everything will be the same except for one thing."

"What's that, Papa?" I asked through my tears.

"It's that I hope you've learned a very painful, but valuable lesson." He paused for emphasis. "The lesson is that we are punished when we do wrong, if not by others, then by our own consciences."

He stopped to let this sink in. Then he looked over to our teachers.

"Thank you, Mrs. Barter, Miss Woodhouse, for your concern. I'll see that Alberta and Eva are properly chastised later at home."

We knew he meant in the smokehouse with a brush broom.

Miss Woodhouse spoke now. "Girls, would you step out into the hall please? I want to have a word with your father."

"Yes'm." We stepped outside the office, but I left the door cracked and could hear their conversation.

"Mr. Wilson, for a long time now I've been hoping to meet with you about the girls, and I'm sorry it had to come to this before we could do so."

"Yes?" asked Papa.

Miss Woodhouse continued. "I'm aware, Mr. Wilson, that your daughters lost their mother only recently, and I think you should take into consideration that their actions may stem in part from that."

'Please go on," said Papa.

"The girls are feeling the lack of a mother more than you probably realize, Mr. Wilson. Not that your mother doesn't do a fine job, of course, but ... I hope, Mr. Wilson, that you don't feel that I am meddling in your affairs. I speak because, as Eva's teacher, I love her and am concerned for her."

"No, no, that's all right, Miss Woodhouse. I can sense you have the girls' welfare in mind. Speak out."

"Mr. Wilson, I think your girls are feeling lost these days. They no longer get the special love and attention they once received from their mother. And you are so often away. By giving out these presents, isn't it possible, they were simply trying to win back some of the things now missing from their lives? I hope you will forgive my frankness."

"Of course, I do. I hadn't thought of it in such a way, Miss Woodhouse. I appreciate your calling my attention to it."

'If you'll forgive another suggestion, Mr. Wilson, I have one."

"Yes?"

"Ever since school began, Eva has been longing to learn to play the piano. I would be most happy to give her lessons each week after school. Of course, that would be later, after her punishment is over. It would be a chance for her to get some of that attention we are talking about, don't you think?"

"Yes, yes I do. It's kind of you to offer. I will think about it. I'm most grateful for any suggestions from you teachers concerning my daughters' well-being."

"And now I must be going," we heard Papa say. "Thank you once more. I can assure you that nothing like this will ever happen again."

104

Papa reached for the door knob behind him, and I started looking as innocent as possible. Papa came out into the hall and we started off when Miss Woodhouse called after him.

"Mr. Wilson, I know this is probably an inopportune time for me to be asking, but your sister, Tess, with whom I board, asked me to pass on to you an invitation to dinner on Sunday."

"Delighted! Tell her I'd be delighted. I look forward to seeing you then, Miss Woodhouse. Good day!"

Chapter XI

MY SCRAPBOOK, JANUARY — JUNE, 1916

After the first week of January, Eva and I had finally "worked out" our punishment. Under the direction of Grandmother Wilson, every day after school and all day on Saturdays we had swept and dusted, scrubbed the kitchen floor, set the tables and washed and dried the dishes, peeled apples and potatoes, ironed the flat items, fed the animals — even plucked chickens. Every day we had to listen to Granddaddy read some verses from the Bible, looking at us very sternly, and talking to us about how a "good name is more to be desired than great riches." But once that was over, Eva got permission to start taking lessons from Miss Woodhouse. She did this every Monday at the piano in the school auditorium, and

I was instructed to sit quietly and wait for her while doing my lessons.

The second Monday Miss Woodhouse brought me something to look at. It was her scrapbook, she explained to me, which she had kept since school days. On its pages she had pasted her report cards, party invitations and favors, letters and post cards, Valentines and Christmas greetings, copies of her favorite poems, colorful cuttings from magazines, clippings from newspapers, pressed flowers and leaves, even photographs. It was beautiful! I begged Papa to buy me a composition book at the store so that I could make one, too. And to show that I was forgiven, he did. My first entry was a newspaper clipping about Papa's new business.

From the Weston Journal:
January 19
The Crescent Box and Lumber Company, dealer in building materials, may be regarded as one of our county's most important new enterprises. A large plant is now being erected near the Norfolk and Western station at Pine Hill.

Mr. William A. Wilson, president, is chief promoter of the enterprise. In addition to manufacturing and dealing in building material, the Crescent Box and Lumber company will manufacture boxes and cases for canned goods which are to be shipped to eastern cities after supplying the local trade.

Mr. Wilson is a native of Pine Hill. He is widely known throughout this section of the state as one of the best posted men on building materials in the Piedmont area. Years of experience in the lumber business have fitted him well for the management of so important an enterprise.

It was just too bad that the news of the world was on the other side of that clipping, which caused Granddaddy to be "greatly perturbed," Grandmother told me after she had calmed him down. She smoothed things over by making the rule that I could have the old newspaper only after the new one arrived. Also, I always had to ask for permission to use the big scissors. She said she would let me keep on making paste out of flour.

Then I had a wonderful idea! As we walked home from school, I told Eva. I said, "While you were having your lesson I got this wonderful idea.!"

"I don't want to hear it," said Eva firmly.

"But why, Eva?" I asked. "Don't you love Miss Woodhouse? This idea is about her! She is so kind to us, so thoughtful, so loving, and smart, too, that wouldn't she make a good mother?"

Eva looked doubtfully at me. "A good mother to who?"

"To us!" I crowed in triumph. "If we can get Papa to marry her, she could be our mother."

Eva kept plodding along, but I could see her getting used to the idea and even liking it.

"But what can we do?" asked Eva plaintively. "We're just children."

I already had our first move planned.

"Well, I happen to know that next week Aunt Nella is having a rook party at her house. Why couldn't we work it so that Papa takes Miss Woodhouse?"

"But how?" Eva wanted to know.

"Why couldn't we get Papa to pick up Miss Woodhouse to show her his new car?"

The talk of Pine Hill was Papa's new Ford touring car.

He was going to Weston to pick it up on Friday, and then we, and everybody for miles around, would get to actually see it.

"How do we do that?"

"Maybe we could get Grandmother Wilson to sort of suggest it to Papa," I said.

"Well, all right, but you do the asking. I'm tired of being your dupe!"

I got my opportunity that afternoon while we were getting supper ready. Grandmother was cutting out biscuits when I made my move.

"Grandmother, did you know that poor Miss Woodhouse hasn't got a way to Aunt Nella's party?"

"Oh, I shouldn't think that would be a problem, Bert. She can certainly ride there with your Aunt Tess and Uncle Olin. Aren't they going?" Grandmother asked.

"Uh, yes ma'm, but Miss Woodhouse has been so nice to us that Eva and I thought she might like to ride in Papa's new car," I blurted out, all my plans for delicacy abandoned.

Grandmother finished the biscuits and wiped the flour from her hands with her apron. "Why, that's a thoughtful idea, Bert! I'll try to suggest it to your Papa."

Grandmother would never know how easily she had fallen into our trap!

Friday finally came, and the whole family assembled at Granddaddy's by late afternoon, eager to see Papa's new automobile. Every time we thought we heard him coming, we would all go out on the porch and strain our eyes down the Cedar Row, but no Papa!

This happened about ten times before it really was Papa coming up the road! Oh, how nattily dressed he was in his Sunday suit with his felt hat tipped a little rakishly. The car was magnificent, so grandly shiny and new, with Papa perched up on the seat like a monarch surveying his kingdom from above.

He took us all for rides down the Cedar Row, beginning with Grandmother and Granddaddy who held on to whatever they could find with iron grips. Then all the uncles and aunts rode, exclaiming at the speed and the ease of operation of it all. Then at last the four of us. It was scary at first, the noise and speed, but it was so exciting to be up there with Papa with the air and the ground rushing past.

The car was the talk of Pine Hill for weeks, and Grandmother must have done her part well for we heard from quite a number of folks that Papa and Miss Woodhouse were seen later driving about together in the new Ford touring car.

From the Dan's Grove Messenger:
Pine Hill Pickings, January 26

A delightful evening of winter entertainment was enjoyed lately at the home of Mr. and Mrs. Dwight Peabody when they welcomed the young people of the community to several tables of progressive rook. After the games, Mrs. Peabody served delicious hot chocolate, sandwiches, and pie with whipped cream and cherries.

High score for the evening was made by local businessman, Will Wilson, who was awarded a tin of mints. The consolation prize, a perfume atomizer, fell to Miss Bess Woodhouse, primary teacher at Pine Hill School.

For Valentine's Day at school our teachers gave out paper and let us make valentines for our friends with scissors and paste. We had a big box decorated with red crepe paper and white doilies, and all of us deposited our valentines there. Our teachers gave out the valentines on February 14, and served us heart-shaped cookies they had made themselves.

This is the valentine from Johnny Lee that I pasted in:

Pigs love pumpkins,
Hogs love squash,
I love you, by gum,
By gosh.

When our school announced plans to put on a play in March, I had another idea which I shared with Eva. "You and I have to get parts in this play, Eva! We just have to!"

"But I don't want to be in the play, Bert," said Eva.

"You don't have a choice, Eva. Can't you see what a good opportunity this will be for us to get Papa and Miss Woodhouse together? He'll have to come to the schoolhouse to see the play, and she will be there directing it, can't you see?"

"But I don't want to get up in front of people and recite. Even if Papa will be there," declared Eva.

"Eva, don't you know there are some things we have to do in life whether we want to or not, and this is one of those things. You have to!" I fixed her with my gimlet eye, and she knew I meant business, and that I would pinch her if she didn't say yes.

From the Dan's Grove Messenger:

Pine Hill Pickings, March 9

The biggest attraction of the season, "A Poor Married Man," was presented last night at the Pine Hill school auditorium. Starring was Art Wilson as the poor married man, a part that took ginger and pep which Arthur has very much of; Miss Delia Wilson as the first bride; Miss Alberta Wilson as the little wife; and Miss Eva Wilson as the little college reporter. Although it was Miss Eva Wilson's first appearance on the stage, she was one of its ablest and most attractive actresses.

I had talked Delia and Art into helping us. They grumbled at all the extra work memorizing, but soon got in the spirit of it and enjoyed being at the center of a lot of attention.

And it worked out perfectly the night of the play. We got through it without making any big blunders, and afterwards in the crush of congratulations around us, I saw Papa talking with Miss Woodhouse over in a corner where they were out of the crowd. They were laughing together at something and really enjoying themselves when Val and Alex ran up. I wanted to go over and get them so that Papa and Miss Woodhouse would have time to themselves, but just at that moment Aunt Sadie came to get us for the trip home, saying that we had Sunday School early the next morning, and Grandmother Wilson had said we must go. There was no use arguing.

But I had a most pleasant surprise when I got hold of the newspaper a week later. This is what I read:

From the Dan's Grove Messenger:
Pine Hill Pickings, March 16

Pine Hill citizens welcomed a few days of spring as roads dried out enough so they were able to get out of town with their cars. A new road from Pine Hill by way of Dillard to Virginia is now under construction.

Mr. Will Wilson took the opportunity to motor to Weston carrying as his passengers the principal of Pine Hill School, Mr. C.D. Chesterton, and two of his teachers, Miss Bess Woodhouse and Mrs. S.T. Barter, on a trip to buy educational supplies for the school.

From the Dan's Grove Messenger:
Pine Hill Pickings, March 23

The Women's Society of the Pine Hill Baptist Church met Sunday afternoon at the home of Mrs. Rupert Wilson. After devotions, the program was in the charge of Miss Bess Woodhouse, who gave an interesting and highly informative talk about her hometown of Boone's Rest. Tradition has it that the great pioneer, Daniel Boone, camped nearby at a pure spring for a few days, breaking his long march across the Alleghenies. Miss Woodhouse described the lovely scenery to be viewed from Boone's Rest, with the Blue Ridge Mountains to the north and west, and the rolling foothills dotted with fine homes and rich plantations to the south and east.

From the Dan's Grove Messenger:
Pine Hill Pickings, April 6

Our community has shared bountifully in the national

prosperity and has scarcely been touched by the wave of "hard times" felt keenly in other sections. Tobacco, corn, and wheat are the chief products of our farms, and all these crops are produced in abundance. In addition, our vegetable and poultry products find an outlet through the markets of Weston. We are justly proud of our community!

From the Dan's Grove Messenger:
Pine Hill Pickings, April 13

Masters Valentine and Alex Wilson, sons of Mr. Will Wilson and grandsons of Andrew Jackson Wilson, with whom they reside, got the fright of their young lives last week when the unhorsed buggy in which they were playing ran away with them on a steep slope of their grandfather's pasture, and plummeted to the bottom where it was smashed to pieces on a rock. Valentine and Alex were able to jump to safety just in time.

When I told Miss Woodhouse about this at school on Monday, she was horrified. "Oh, no!" she cried out, holding both hands to her heart, "Your poor brothers! Were they hurt? Didn't it scare them half to death? Oh, I want to send them something nice. Better yet, I'll take them something this afternoon on my way home. Do you think that would be all right with your grandmother?"

She rummaged in her desk and came up with a paper sack which she said contained licorice candy. Did I think they would like that?

And that was how Miss Woodhouse happened to go home with us that afternoon. Eva and I left school floating on clouds of bliss at being in the company of our school's sweetest and dearest teacher. Our classmates were hanging behind us respectfully, trying hard to overhear our every exchange. All too soon we reached home and ran to find Grandmother who fetched Val and Alex, (cleaning them up beforehand with a wet rag). We all sat in the parlor and after Miss Woodhouse had given Val and Alex their treat and inquired about their frightening experience, she got around to telling Grandmother how Eva and I were doing in school, and how Eva was progressing on the piano. Eva was captivated by all this attention, even if it had been the result of Val's and Alex's accident. Grandmother sent Aunt Sadie to the icehouse for ice, and we all had glasses of delicious canned grape juice.

Then unexpectedly for the middle of the week, we heard Papa's car chugging up the road out front, and suddenly he appeared in the parlor door, wiping his forehead with a handkerchief and looking flustered, I guess, because he was in his overalls.

"Will," said Grandmother, "Miss Woodhouse is here! Come in and have a glass of grape juice with us."

"If you'll give me a minute to clean up, I'll do just that, Mama," he said, and reappeared in a few minutes looking spiffier. Then Miss Woodhouse had to tell again how scared she was when she heard about the boys' misadventure, and how she just had to come bring them a treat — she hoped it was all right to interrupt the work day. And then she looked at the watch which she kept hanging around her neck on a silver chain and stated that she believed she had overstayed her welcome and must go at once. Grandmother rose and added, "Miss Woodhouse, I wonder if you could come to dinner next Sunday? We would be so pleased if you would."

"Why, thank you, Mrs. Wilson. I'll look forward to that."

Papa smiled at Miss Woodhouse. "I'd be happy to drive you home," he offered.

"That would be lovely, Mr. Wilson, if it wouldn't be out of your way."

The two drove off in the Ford touring car, leaving Eva and me to clutch each other, overcome with giggles of joy and delight.

From the Dan's Grove Messenger:
Pine Hill Pickings, May 25

On the 17th day of May, Pine Hill School was brought to a close with the best commencement this school has had for many years. Present enrollment stands at 126 with an average daily attendance of 100. Every child in the district between the ages of 8 and 12 is enrolled. It is to be hoped that requirements can be met for placing the school on the accredited list by the time the fall term begins.

There will be a change in the faculty of the primary department. Miss Bess Woodhouse will be leaving, but will return next fall as Mrs. W.A. Wilson! Congratulations, Mr. and Mrs. Wilson!

My last entry for awhile was a wedding invitation postmarked Boone's Rest, May 28.

Mr. and Mrs. S. J. Woodhouse

request the pleasure of your company

at the marriage of their daughter,

Mary Elizabeth

to

Mr. William Albert Wilson

on Wednesday afternoon, the twenty-eighth of June,

nineteen hundred and sixteen

at half after two o'clock at their home

Boone's Rest, North Carolina

Chapter XII

HOME TO FERN CLIFF

After dinner the family gathered on the porch just as usual for Sunday, but this time an unusual expectancy hung over the group settling down on the hard rockers and benches, and along the summer-dusty steps.

We were awaiting the arrival of Papa and Miss Woodhouse (I couldn't seem to stop calling her that) who had sent a telegram from Weston (almost causing Grandmother to have heart failure) announcing that they would be picking up Baby Clay on the way home from their honeymoon and would be arriving about two. They had requested that Eva, Val, Alex, and I be ready to depart for our new home.

Naturally, the four of us were practically out of our heads with anticipation. Val and Alex had already run down to the end of the Cedar Row four times, thinking they heard Papa's new Ford touring car coming.

The old covered wagon had been pulled up to the back of the house and loaded with all our belongings, and Eva and I were doing our best to stay clean and neat as Aunt Sadie had urged us.

During the week past she had washed and ironed all our clothes, and she was putting them into our trunks on Saturday when she said, "Well, now, we certainly are going to miss you, but we understand your wanting to be back with your papa and Baby Clay in your own home. Isn't it a blessing that he has found such a nice mama for you all?"

"Yes, m'am," agreed Eva and I.

"Aunt Sadie?" I asked as I handed her a stack of starched petticoats, "Isn't life strange?"

"Yes, Bert, it certainly is *that*," she answered, and I wondered if she were thinking of the fact that she had never grown up, and wondering why it had to happen to *her*.

"I mean," I continued, "in life bad things happen sometimes, and sometimes good things happen."

"Yes, that's the way it seems to go," replied Aunt Sadie, coiling a sash up into a neat little spring.

"Like Mama dying was really, really bad," I went on, "but Papa finding Miss Woodhouse was really, really good. I wonder..."

"Wonder what, my dear?" Aunt Sadie, tucking in a shoe.

"I wonder what would have happened to us if we hadn't come here to be with all of you. It might have been a bad thing. Instead, it was a good thing, our being able to be with you, with Grandmother and Granddaddy, and Delia and Uncle Whit and everybody. Even Art."

"We are just thankful you could," said Aunt Sadie.

119

"A family is one of the good things, isn't it?"

"I know I'm glad I'm a member of one," replied Aunt Sadie briskly. She closed the trunk.

Now Granddaddy opened up the "Messenger" with his usual Sunday flourish. Although the newspaper always came in Friday's mail, Granddaddy would not allow himself even one little peek until the week's work was finished and his Sabbath begun. Except when entertaining guests, he used this time for a perusal of the weekly news.

Granddaddy spent a minute straightening the paper with important crackling sounds and also clearings of his throat in case there was any news he felt he should impart to us. Everyone was respectfully quiet during this time.

Grandmother came out the front door and joined us, having left the kitchen to Molly and Martha. Sitting down, she took up her favorite fan, a palm-leaf one, and began to use it, complaining of the heat of the day.

Granddaddy cleared his throat again, and reported to the group at large: "Here is an item that might interest some of you. Arthur, fetch my glass."

Arthur ran to get the magnifying glass that Granddaddy used to make his reading easier.

"That's better. Now:

"Miss Bess Woodhouse of Boone's Rest and Mr. William Wilson of Pine Hill were married in a beautiful wedding at the home of the bride's parents, Mr. and Mrs. S.J. Woodhouse, at 2:30, June 28, in Boone's Rest.

"The beautiful home was made still more attractive for the occasion with artistic decorations of potted plants and cut flowers, the general color scheme of pink and white having been carried out in varying tones in different rooms of the house.

"Guests were greeted at the door by Mrs. S.J. Woodhouse and were directed into the gift room where an array of handsome and useful gifts attested to the popularity of the young couple.

"Mrs. J.A. Mead sang 'O, Promise Me' after which Miss Ruth Beckmon played Mendelssohn's 'Wedding March.' The impressive ceremony was performed by the Reverend A.F. Hayworth in the softly shaded parlor.

"Following the ceremony, the guests were invited into the dining room where a delicious ice course was served.

"The bride is a very attractive and popular young woman, having hosts of friends in this and other sections of the state. She is a young woman of winning personality and many admirable qualities. For the past year she has been a teacher at the Pine Hill School.

"Mr. Wilson is a popular and successful young man, having been engaged in the lumber and contracting business at Pine Hill for the past ten years. He is now president and general manager of the Crescent Box and Lumber Company.

"Following the reception, Mr. and Mrs. Wilson left for a visit to Weston and are stopping at the Zinzindorf Hotel. After a week they will be at home at their new bungalow, Fern Cliff."

"Fern Cliff?" Grandmother stopped fanning to ask, "what, pray tell, is Fern Cliff?"

I tried to sidle unobtrusively away from the center of the gathering, but Grandmother's eagle eye found me just as I eased behind my tallest uncle.

"Alberta, what is this Fern Cliff?"

"It's just Papa's new house," I replied.

"You mean they plan to call it that ridiculous name?" asked Grandmother, amazed. "That doesn't sound at all like Bess or Will to me."

"Well it's not exactly *their* name for it," I answered truthfully. "It's more like *my* name for it."

"I might have known!" said Grandmother. "Explain yourself."

"Well," I answered slowly, feeling my way along carefully for the most blameless effect, "the day the newspaper correspondent came to talk to Miss Woodhouse about her wedding plans, I was in her classroom helping her pack some school things, and afterwards, all I did was walk out to the road with her, the newspaper lady, I mean, and I merely told her about the house Papa was having built and that it was going to be called Fern Cliff. I made the name up, and I think it's beautiful."

"Bert! It was not your place to do such a thing. Besides, it sounds pretentious," scolded Grandmother.

"I suppose there *are* a few ferns on that cliff," put in Granddaddy dryly, turning to the next page of his newspaper and closing the matter once and for all.

At that moment, we heard a loud chugging and saw a tunnel of red dust rising along the Cedar Row. It was the touring car with Papa and Miss Woodhouse!

Evidently Val and Alex had slipped away again because now they appeared riding the running boards of the car. Miss

Woodhouse cradled Baby Clay in her left arm and held tight onto Alex on one side, and Papa held his arm around Val on the other. Both boys had grins that stretched straight across.

"Hello, hello," everybody was calling as they got up

The family poured down the steps like church letting out, and Eva and I ran out in front of everybody so as to be the first to welcome them home.

VIEWPOINT PRESS, INC.

is proud to announce our next publication

— WALKING RIBBON —

a story of Liberty, NC in 1898.

Maggie is proud of her calf, Ribbon — so proud that she decides to show off her calf around town. They are having a very pleasant stroll through Liberty, when the "Shoo Fly" train comes down the tracks, toot-tooting its whistle. What happens next is not exactly what Maggie had in mind.

This charming and amusing tale is illustrated with watercolors by Elizabeth Macdonald of Jamestown, NC. The art work helps round out the total picture of Liberty, giving the readers a look at the typical small agricultural towns that developed along the railroad.

The simple but compelling story with its lovely full-color paintings will greatly appeal to the reader from Kindergarten age through 4th grade. You will also find that even adult history buffs will appreciate the accuracy of story and art to the period.

Give a child a piece of North Carolina history to cherish!

ALSO, WATCH FOR OUR SERIES

Ms. Monroe's Marvelous Classroom

These entertaining books (with language experience ideas for strengthening your child's reading and writing skills), began with T*he Super, Stupendous, and Tremendously Terrific Show-and-Tell Day* and will continue in the spring with *Nora's Terrible Picture Day*.

The series will contain ten stories, approximately two at each grade level from one to five, as the children in Ms. Monroe's experimental class are growing older. They were chosen to stay together for the five years of elementary school as a way of seeing which situation creates the better learning environment: the same students with the same teacher for five years or the normal shifting of class menbers and teachers for each year. Our stories try to focus on situations that could really occur with schools and children of today.

Because of our dedication to children and children's causes, 1% of the profit of each of the series books (beginning with the second) will be donated to a related cause. The percentage from the sale of *Nora's Terrible Picture Day* will go to Motheread, a literacy program based in Raleigh, NC. The author of each book will select the recipient.

To request a listing of available books, contact:
Viewpoint Press, P.O. Box 430-B
Pleasant Garden, NC 27313
or **email**:   Vpressbks@worldnet.att.net

126

Viewpoint Press, Inc. — dedicated to the production of the highest quality books for children of all ages.

Reading with a child is one of the greatest expressions of love.

Visit our Web Site:

http://members.tripod.com/~viewpointpress

Enter our contests for our friends 12 years and under. Some require artwork, some are poetry, some are writing. Try it and see if **YOU** can be a prize winner!